## WHAT THE <u>REAL</u> CRITICS HAVE TO SAY

*My gran bought me your book as a birthday present.
I have no idea what I did to upset her*

– Lauren, aged 7, NT

*You have many things in common with Roald Dahl,
but writing good stories isn't one of them*

– Brendan, aged 14, SA

*I read your book while I was recovering
from appendicitis in hospital. I'm not sure
which experience was most painful*

– Gabrielle, aged 8, ACT

*My teacher caught me reading your book during
Maths. She was going to give me a detention,
but reckoned I'd suffered enough*

– Jasmin, aged 10, VIC

*Your new book is pitiful, pathetic and poorly
written – a huge improvement on your last*

– Mya, still in the womb, NSW

# BLACKY
# BLASTS
# BACK!

## ON THE TAIL
## OF THE
## TASSIE TIGER

ALLEN&UNWIN

First published in 2010

Allen & Unwin
83 Alexander Street
Crows Nest NSW 2065
Australia
 *Phone*  (612) 8425 0100
   *Fax*  (612) 9906 2218
 *Email*  info@allenandunwin.com
   *Web*  www.allenandunwin.com

National Library of Australia Cataloguing-in-Publication entry
    Jonsberg, Barry, 1951–
    Blacky blasts back: on the tail of the Tassie tiger
    For primary school age.
    ISBN: 978 174237 223 5 (pbk.)
    A823.4

Cover and text design by Bruno Herfst

This book was printed in November 2009 at McPherson's Printing Group,
76 Nelson Street, Maryborough, Victoria, 3465, Australia.
www.mcphersonsprinting.com.au

www.allenandunwin.com/kids

*For Freddi, Tris and Damien*

My name is Marcus, but you can call me Boris the Impaler.

Hell child.

Born-to-be-wild.

Ripper-off-of-chooks'-heads-with-his-teeth.

Or just plain Marc if you prefer.

It was Monday morning and I sat at the breakfast table, glowering at my sister Rose. For some reason, Mum had neglected to provide a live chook whose head I could bite off, so I was forced to settle for a round of toast.

I tore off a jammy chunk, drool dripping from my chin. Then I let out a low growl, my eyes hard pinpricks of pure evil. Wickedness ran through my veins. My muscles bunched and tensed. Fingers, itching for destruction, clawed at the tablecloth.

'Are you okay, Marcus?' said Mum, putting a milk jug in front of Rose. 'You look constipated.'

I gave an icy chuckle, but then a stabbing pain shot through my ankle and I choked on my toast. Rose had kicked me under the table. She'd been doing that a lot recently. My chuckle turned into a strangled whimper. I coughed violently and a plug of bread exploded from my throat, travelled like a speeding bullet across the table, ricocheted off the milk jug and pinged Rose between the eyes.

Mum shrieked.

Rose slumped to the floor, eyes rolling back in her head.

Amid the confusion, I grabbed my backpack and scuttled out the door.

School beckoned and Boris had impaling to do.


Assembly. A perfect opportunity for raising hell.

It is the custom at my school for seven hundred kids to sit cross-legged on the gym floor and fall asleep while teachers drone on about nothing. Today Miss Dowling, our Principal, was the main event, so I waited while the warm-up acts finished their turns. If I was going to do something spectacularly bad – something gut-wrenchingly terrible – it would have to be when Miss D was in full flow.

Words floated across the gym and died before they reached my ears. I was lost in my own head, planning. My first idea was to stand when the Prinny was slotting into top gear, and drop an amazingly loud and fruity fart. Trouble is, that's not something you can produce on demand. I wasn't confident I wouldn't just strain, turn beetroot red and poop my pants.

Nasty, yes. But more embarrassing than destructive. Not the behaviour of a devil child.

Maybe I could just yell out something really offensive.

Pull the pigtails of random year-seven girls. Projectile vomit on Miss Dowling's shoes.

I was running through the options when I realised the time had come. Miss Dowling had the microphone and was pacing the stage. I hadn't even noticed her move into the spotlight. And I had absolutely no idea what she was talking about. But what I *did* know was that this was the time to act. Just leap up and do something really, really bad. Trust my instinct. Let the evil work through me. Now or never. Do it, Marcus. *Do it!*

I jumped to my feet and Miss Dowling paused in her flow of words. She looked straight at me. My knees trembled but I opened my mouth. I would have been fascinated to know what I was going to say, but I never got the chance. She spoke first.

'Splendid, Marcus,' she said. 'What a good start to our School Community Project! Those pensioners will be so grateful for your help with their gardens. I hope the rest of you are as impressed as I am by Marcus's selflessness. Five gold stars!'

My mouth closed and opened again. I did a fabulous impersonation of a goldfish for a few moments. Then I sat down.

Lunch. A perfect time for mayhem.

Normally I take a packed lunch, but this morning I'd left it in the fridge. After braining Rose with the lump of half-chewed toast, I had made a hasty retreat. So I searched my pockets for shrapnel and came up with enough to buy a hot dog from the canteen. A double helping of tomato sauce dripped over my fingers. I chewed at the roll, but left the pale sausage intact.

Miss Monkhouse was the teacher on yard duty. This was a stroke of luck. Miss Monkhouse is the scariest teacher in the school. She regularly chews up students and spits them out. She's as tough as a sumo wrestler, only larger. She's never smiled and doesn't seem inclined to risk it. She can maim at fifty metres with one blow of her tongue.

Miss Monkhouse leaned against a pillar at the side of the canteen, blotting out the sun and gazing at the kids in the yard. She had her back to me. I balanced the dripping hot dog in my hand and edged closer. The broad expanse of her neck made a perfect target. I couldn't miss. I could imagine the moment of impact. The splat of the hot dog, the splatter of flying sauce, even … maybe, just maybe … the sausage sliding down her neckline and lodging in the small of her back. If her back had anywhere that was small.

I took a deep breath and let my missile fly.

You know how I said I couldn't miss?

I was wrong.

The hot dog hit the pillar she was leaning against and rebounded. The impact must have drawn her attention, because she turned around. Just in time to see the hot dog bounce on the edge of a rubbish bin, teeter for a moment on the rim like a basketball making up its mind whether to be a basket or not, and then drop neatly into its depths.

You could have practised that trick a thousand times and never pulled it off. Miss Monkhouse gazed at me.

'Good boy, Marcus,' she said. For a second I thought she was going to smile. I think she tried, but the muscles must have seized up through lack of use. 'You wouldn't believe how many children just drop their rubbish on the ground. Well done. Five gold stars!'

Science. Last lesson of the day. Perfect for mischief.

Chemicals, Bunsen burners, test tubes. The Spawn of Satan couldn't have asked for a better environment for creating havoc. No way I could fail. Like shooting fish in a barrel. Easy-peasy lemon-squeezy.

I'd learned something that day. KISS. Keep It Simple, Stupid. Yes, creating a bomb out of a chemical reaction might do the trick, but I'm not crash hot at Science. More likely I'd mix up some stuff and discover a cure for cancer. Incinerate Mr Scott's desk with a Bunsen burner? Too time-consuming. Dissect a student? Too messy.

So I decided to throw a beaker full of something nasty-smelling at the wall. A distant wall. I didn't want anyone hurt by flying glass. It was absolutely foolproof. Suspension guaranteed.

It all went according to plan. Up to a point. The teacher's back was turned. My beaker was full of a bright purple liquid and smelled like a dunny at the annual Diarrhoea Sufferers' Convention. I put my right foot behind me to get more power into the throw. But before I could release the beaker, a number of things happened:

A   Mr Scott turned round.

B   I caught my foot on a stool.

C   Tonia Niven, a small and exceptionally clumsy girl, reached over the Bunsen burner to pick up her beaker and set the arm of her dress on fire.

D  I lost my balance.

E  I fell on top of Tonia, my beaker dropping onto the bench where, miraculously, it didn't break or even spill a drop of its contents.

F  Tonia and I rolled on the floor for a few horribly embarrassing seconds and when we got to our feet her sleeve was smoking gently.

There was a stunned silence. Mr Scott rushed up and examined Tonia's arm. Then he turned to me.

'Marcus. That was the bravest thing I have ever seen.'

'But sir…'

'No modesty, Marcus. I saw it all. Tonia could have been badly burned. But you didn't hesitate. Just threw yourself onto her and put out the fire. Twenty gold stars, Marcus! And that's just for starters. Miss Dowling will know about your heroism.'

Things couldn't get any worse.

Tonia gazed into my eyes. Hers were shining with a sloppy, gooey sludge of emotions.

'You're my hero, Marcus,' she breathed through buck teeth. 'Will you be my boyfriend?'

I was wrong. Things *could* get worse.

It was a depressed Boris the Impaler who trudged home from school that afternoon.

How could it all go so horribly wrong? How could I stuff up so monumentally? My plan had been simple enough. Get a reputation for being a top-notch drongo, a prize-winning dropkick, a grade-A loser. Instead, I was probably going to be made Head Boy and crowned Young Australian of the Year. Obviously I couldn't get anything right. Or do I mean 'wrong'? Hopeless. Absolutely hopeless.

I opened my front door, screamed and fell to the floor clutching my ankle. I didn't get time to rub at the fire raging there, because two hands grabbed my left wrist and gave it a vicious Chinese burn. Now two parts of my anatomy were throbbing.

Rose's face loomed before me. You'd think I'd suffered enough.

'Try to blind me, would you, Mucus?' she hissed. 'I'll teach you to try to blind me!'

But she didn't give me the promised lesson in blinding. She simply sawed away with renewed vigour at my wrist, gave my ankle another kick in exactly the same place as before and left me on the floor, writhing in pain.

All in all, it had been a great Monday.

I need to explain.

Let me start with a confession. Nobody calls me Boris the Impaler. My real name is Marcus Hill, a.k.a. Marcus the Sook. I'm just an average Year Seven student and I *never* get in trouble at school. Not even when I try. So you're probably wondering why I went to such lengths to cause trouble. The answer lies in a conversation I'd had the previous Friday with the Principal…

'But Miss Dowling, I want to go!'

The Principal sat behind her desk and cradled her chin on interlaced fingers. She wore a brightly coloured dress and a kind expression.

'I understand, Marcus,' she said, 'but this school camp isn't open to everyone. I've already explained that. It's only available to our special boys unit. And it's not really going to be fun, if you want to know the truth. It's all about developing leadership skills, building resilience and taking responsibility for your own actions. There will be hardship involved. Survival techniques. Tough bushwalks. Camping out in harsh conditions.'

She *had* explained this. The special boys unit is composed of six or seven students in my year group who have severe behavioural problems. The kind of boys who act first and think afterwards. A long time afterwards. Sometimes not at all. My mate Dylan is one of them. He was a nightmare at primary school. He's a nightmare in secondary school. But he's also the best friend anyone could have.

I tried the goody-two-shoes sook approach.

'But Miss Dowling,' I whined. 'I've never been to Tasmania and I really want to go. How about if I promise to be very, very good?'

'You're missing the point, Marcus. The boys on this special camp are going precisely because they aren't very, very good.'

'Okay. I promise to be very, very bad.'

Miss Dowling brushed a speck of dust from the shining surface of her desk and got to her feet. This meeting was drawing to a close.

'I'm sorry, Marcus. I really am. But the funding for this project – which is provided by the education department – is very specific. Only the special boys group. And you are not part of that.'

*I'm average boys group*, I thought. It's not fair. If you're bad you get rewarded. If you're average you get zilch.

And that's when the idea popped into my head. If you had to be a drongo to get on this trip, then a drongo I'd become. It couldn't be too hard. The members of the special boys group found it a cinch. Didn't have to put in any effort at all.

As I left Miss Dowling's office, my mind was made up. I was going to join the ranks of the nightmare kids.

Boris the Impaler was born.

And he died the very next school day.

I dragged his aching body into my bedroom and closed the door. Then I hopped to my bed and examined my swollen ankle. Rose might be the sister from hell and a total loser, but she's a precision ankle-kicker. That was three times today. And all on the same spot. I lay back on the bed and closed my eyes. My plan had seemed so foolproof and now it lay in tatters. How was I going to get on the camp?

You see, it wasn't just a question of *wanting* to go. I *had* to be there. I just had to. And time was running out. The ferry trip to Tassie was the coming Thursday. Three days away. I had to do something, and do it now. But the more I thought, the more hopeless it seemed.

A rattle of stones on my window drew me from the start of a doze. I hobbled over to the window and opened it.

Dylan slid in.

I've already mentioned Dyl. My best mate. A small, wiry kid with a serious cola addiction and no discernible fear. Dyl could have knocked on the front door, but he doesn't do anything normal. He just likes throwing stones at breakable things. There was a time when Mum wouldn't let him into the house at all. She regarded Dylan as a small but powerful weapon of mass destruction. But he came with us on holiday last Christmas and since then Mum has taken a shine to him.

Dyl pulled a cola can from his jacket pocket, popped the ring pull and took a deep swig.

'Wassup, Marc?' he said.

'Nothing good, mate,' I replied. 'Nothing good.'

I explained how my day had gone. Dyl isn't in any of my classes. Since we both started at secondary school he spends his days with the other members of the special boys unit in a classroom at the far end of the school, where the screams and sounds of breaking objects can't be heard by the rest of us. I've asked Dyl what they do in there all day, but he can never remember.

I read something once about some subatomic particles existing for only one billionth of a second. They still last longer than Dyl's memory.

Anyway, judging by his teacher's appearance, the main area of the special boys' curriculum involves inducing nervous breakdowns in adults. Mr Crannitch used to be young, dark-haired and energetic. Like us, he joined the school at the start of the academic year. But after one term of dealing with Dyl and the others, he's now a shambling, grey-haired, drooling dude who mutters to himself and twitches constantly.

I didn't spare Dyl any of the hideous experiences I'd been through.

'Wow,' he said when I was done. 'So are you going to be Tonia's boyfriend? She's kinda scary, man.'

'Of course not, ya dill,' I replied. 'That's not the worst thing to have happened today.'

'You sure? I can't imagine anything worse.'

'Dylan,' I said with a sigh. 'The worst thing is that I can't see any way to get on that school camp with you. Miss Dowling won't hear of it.'

'Hey,' said Dyl. 'I've got it! Why don't you just act really badly at school? You know, get into trouble, get transferred to the special boys unit with me.'

I sighed again. When Dyl's your best mate you do a lot of sighing.

'Don't you ever listen, Dyl? I've just finished explaining that that was what I was trying to achieve today.'

'Sorry, mate. What did you say? I wasn't listening.'

I sighed.

There's something else I need to explain and I must warn you the next bit is difficult to believe. You see, there was a good reason why I needed to get to Tasmania within the next few days. Possibly you thought I wanted to be with my mate, but that's not the case at all.

Don't get me wrong. I'd do anything for Dylan and he'd do anything for me. But I could live without him for a week, which was how long the camp was lasting. It's not as if we're joined at the hip. Plus, the other kids who were going weren't exactly a barrel of laughs. For example, there was John, a specimen with the build of a basketball player and the personality of a serial killer. His speciality was torture. Other kids if he could get them, but failing that, any passing butterfly would do. Then there was Brodie. He made John look like a candidate for sainthood. And then there was Kyle …

This would be like going on holiday with a pack of rabid dogs. Only more dangerous. I could do without it.

But Blacky hadn't given me a choice …

I hate to give the impression I'm telling this story backwards, but can we go back to the Thursday before my pointless interview with Miss Dowling? I promise I won't do it again, otherwise we'll be finishing this story with my birth. Although that's a pretty spectacular event from my point of view, I doubt you'd find it fascinating.

Thursday evening. It hadn't been the greatest evening, mainly because Rose had spent dinner repeatedly kicking me under the table. It is Rose's mission in life to make mine miserable and she pursues it with enormous energy and considerable success. You might wonder why I don't simply dob her in to my parents, show them the bruises and gloat while they give her a sound thrashing with a length of lead piping.

Okay. A grounding, at least.

The thing is, they wouldn't believe me. As far as they're concerned, Rose can do no wrong. If they discovered my sister disembowelling me with a rusty tin opener, they'd assume she was performing emergency lifesaving surgery and double her pocket money.

It's not fair.

So I limped into my bedroom and had a go at my Maths homework.

*A man is filling a tank with water at a rate of 30 litres a minute. The tank is 3.5 metres long, 4.5 metres wide and 6 metres deep. However, the tank has a leak exactly halfway up and when the water reaches this level it escapes at a rate of 5 litres a minute. Bearing in mind that 1 cubic metre contains 1000 litres, how long would it take for the tank to overflow?*

I thought about it.

'*Never,*' I wrote, '*because only a complete moron with a criminal disregard for water conservation would carry on filling a tank when it was spewing out 5 litres a second through a leak.*'

Satisfied I'd aced that one, I had a shower, brushed my teeth and got into bed. I was going to do some reading, but I was tired out from dinner. It's exhausting having your shins hammered with steel-capped boots. So I turned off the lamp and snuggled down into my doona.

I don't know if this has ever happened to you. You drift into that cosy state of pre-sleep, suspended in warmth. You fall deeper and deeper into a blissful void. Your breathing relaxes into a peaceful rhythm.

And then a cold wet nose is thrust into your ear.

Okay. It must be just me.

I yelled and jumped out of bed in one movement, like one of those vertical take-off military jets. I nearly scraped the ceiling. Just as well I'd only recently been to the bathroom. Otherwise *I'd* have been leaking at the rate of 5 litres a minute.

I pressed back against the wall, peered through the darkness towards my bed and prayed I was in the throes of a nightmare.

'Tickle my bum with a feather, tosh,' came a voice in my head. 'You scared the living daylights out of me, you twonk!'

I took a step nearer the bed.

'Blacky?' I breathed.

'Who were you expecting, bucko? Barack Obama?'

I turned on the bedside light.

A small, scruffy, dirty-white dog sat on my pillow. It looked at me through pink-rimmed eyes.

'Wotcha, mush,' said the dog.

Now this is the bit you'll find hard to believe.

Blacky is a talking dog.

Well, he can't actually *talk*. He's not in demand as an after-dinner speaker, and he'd flunk an English oral outright. But he *can* communicate. Only with me, though.

It works this way. His voice appears in my head and my voice, it seems, appears in his. It's called telepathy: the ability to talk to someone through their thoughts. According to Blacky, I am one of only four people in Australia to have this gift and there aren't many animals who can do what Blacky does. Just thought I'd let you know that while you *could* spend hours talking to a pot-bellied pig, you're unlikely to get anything out of it other than a headache

and a reputation for being one snag short of a barbie.

Blacky doesn't turn up often, but when he does it's because he has a mission for me. An animal somewhere needs my help. So far, I've successfully completed two missions. Or rather, me and Dyl have. Dylan is the only other person who knows about Blacky. We are an ecological double-act, tidying up messes that human beings have created. But you'll understand more as the story goes on …

'Blacky!' I yelled in my head. 'It's great to see you.'

He cocked his head.

'Of course it is, tosh,' he replied. 'You're only human. Some would say *barely* human.'

I wanted to throw my arms around him, but stopped myself just in time. Blacky doesn't do affection. In fact, he's the grumpiest, meanest, worst-tempered, rudest creature I've ever known. And I've spent my entire life with Rose, remember.

'What's the mission, Blacky?' I said.

'What makes you think there *is* a mission, tosh?' he replied. 'Maybe I'm just passing through and felt like chatting with an old friend.'

'Really?'

'No. You're not an old friend. You're a brain-dead bozo. Anyway, there's a mission.'

'What is it?'

Blacky scratched an ear and gave his bum a quick lick. That reminded me. I knew something was different. Every other time I'd found Blacky in my room he'd been accompanied by a foul smell. You see, Blacky has a fart problem.

17

Well, *he* doesn't consider it a problem, but anything living within a two-kilometre radius does. I've seen flowers wilt, birds plummet from the sky and grown men weep and lose the will to live.

'Changed my diet, tosh,' said Blacky. I'd forgotten there was no such thing as a private thought with him around. 'But, if you're feeling nostalgic, I'm sure I could manage a small one ...'

'No!' I yelled. 'It's okay, seriously. Tell me about the mission instead.'

'Ah, the mission, mush. 'Fraid I can't tell you. That's on a need-to-know basis.'

'What do you mean, "a need-to-know basis"? If you've got a mission for me, don't I need to know what it is?'

'Only those who need to know, know. Those who don't need to know, don't know. You aren't on a need-to-know basis, so you don't know and I don't need to tell you what you don't need to know. You need to know this.'

I let the words roll around in my head for a while, but it was obvious I wasn't going to make any sense of them.

'So who does need to know, then?' I asked.

'You don't need to know that. That's also on a need-to-know basis.'

I threw myself on the bed. I'd forgotten how annoying the smelly hound could be.

'So let me get this right,' I said. 'You've got a mission for me, but I don't need to know what it is? How am I supposed to complete it, then? And if you tell me that's on a need-to-know basis, I should warn you I'm liable to insert my foot up your backside.'

Blacky sniffed inside my head.

'Charming,' he said. 'Why is it that humans resort to violence when they don't get their own way?'

'I can't tell you,' I replied. 'That's on a need-to-know basis.'

'Be in Tasmania by the end of next week,' said Blacky. 'When you're there, I will give you more information.'

*More* information?

I laughed.

'You just don't get it, do you, Blacky?' I said. 'You really have no idea how the world of humans works. Well, here is something you *do* need to know. I am twelve years old, *tosh*. I can't throw a few clothes into a bag, book a flight on the internet using my credit card, order a taxi and take off to Tassie at the drop of a hat. I am forced to eat all the green beans on my plate, wear matching socks and wash behind my ears. Now, I have no idea why the dark side of my ears should get particularly dirty. Maybe that's on a need-to-know basis. But I do it because I have to do what I'm told. I can't go to Tasmania, Blacky. I've got to go to school and wash the dishes on Tuesdays and Fridays. This is my world. I can't change it.'

There was silence for about thirty seconds.

'I understand one thing, tosh,' said Blacky. 'I understand your school is organising a trip to Tasmania. I even know your dropkick mate Dylan is going.'

I was tempted to ask him *how* he knew, but I was worried he'd tell me I didn't need to know. Anyway, he carried on talking.

'This is the most important mission I have ever set you, mush. The other two are trivial in comparison. This one

will alter history. So I suggest you find a way of getting on that trip. If you are serious about helping the world, you'll be on that boat.'

I was shaken. True, Blacky wasn't above pulling the wool over my eyes. If he thought it would help him he'd shear the sheep and knit the wool himself. The last mission I completed was proof of that. But, somehow, I knew he was telling the truth. This mission was going to be the most important thing I'd done so far. I felt it in my bones.

Of course, knowing this didn't mean I was any closer to getting on the trip. The greatest drawback of having a dirty-white dog as your main informant is the difficulty of getting anyone to take you seriously. 'I need to go to Tassie, Miss Dowling. A small, farting dog told me I was going to change history.' Plus, I was aware the trip was only for the special boys unit. But, then again, I was resourceful. It wasn't impossible, particularly if the stakes were as high as Blacky reckoned.

I turned to tell him all this, but the pillow was empty. I could see my window, open about thirty centimetres.

'Blacky?'

Nothing.

I went to the window and raised the sash. The air outside was chilly. The stars were sharp in the sky.

'I'll try, Blacky,' I yelled in my head. 'I can't do any more than try.'

There was no reply. I watched clouds drift like smoke against the bone-white moon.

'I'll try, Blacky,' I whispered to the night.

At least I don't have to go any further back in time, which is cool. I was starting to confuse myself.

It was Tuesday morning and I felt depressed. Not even a good kicking from Rose could stir me up. The trip was the day after tomorrow! I sat at the breakfast table, my head down. Concentrating. There was no way now I'd be joining Dyl as part of the official school expedition, so I needed to come up with alternative strategies.

When the going gets tough, the tough get going.

Perhaps I'd have to arrive at school on Thursday and stow away on the school bus going to the ferry. Maybe I could pack myself into Dylan's suitcase. Or I could hitch a ride to Tassie. Pretend to be a dwarf and join a travelling circus. Make my own hot-air balloon. Tie a whole bunch of material together and get Blacky to fart into it.

Hopeless.

When the going gets tough, Marcus loses it.

I dragged myself to school. Depressed. Tonia Niven was waiting at the school gates, mouth full of metal, face splattered with freckles and red pigtails sticking out of her head at alarming angles. She gave me a sickly-sweet smile and my mood, not good to start with, plummeted.

I ran.

Another sound reason to get to Tasmania. Though with Tonia you felt Tassie was never going to be far enough away.

The Principal was prowling the schoolyard like a guard dog. I nearly ran her over in my haste to get away from Tonia. She grabbed the straps of my backpack. For a moment my legs and arms were going in a blur while the rest of me stayed still.

'Marcus,' she said. 'Whoa there. Do you still want to go on the camp to Tasmania?'

I allowed my legs and arms to come to rest, like a fan winding down.

'What? Yes, Miss. Yes, I do.'

'A boy has dropped out, which means there is a spare place. Come to my office and I'll give you the necessary forms for your parents to sign. But you must get them back to me by tomorrow morning.'

'No problem, Miss. Thanks. Thanks a lot.' I didn't want to risk asking, but I couldn't help it. 'Miss? You said this was only for boys with behavioural problems. So why are you letting me go?'

'Well, Marcus,' said Miss Dowling, 'it is true that the camp is mainly to help some boys with their social skills. But after the way you've behaved recently – the volunteering to garden for our senior citizens, your heroism in the Science lab – I think you will be an excellent role model for those boys. Show them it's okay to be responsible and caring. Plus, the Education Department has already paid for that place.'

I felt like jumping into the air and yelling. Just when things had appeared impossible, a way had been found. It was fate. Fortune was smiling on me now, instead of pooing in my back pocket. I was so happy I could have kissed Tonia. Luckily, I stopped myself.

'This seems like a tough camp, Marcus,' said Dad.

It was Thursday and the family was sitting down for breakfast. My bags, all packed, were on the floor next to me. Dad was re-reading the information Miss Dowling had given me about the Wilderness Camp.

'I mean, it's a fabulous opportunity,' Dad continued. 'Don't get me wrong. Camping, kayaking, abseiling, fishing, rock-climbing, whitewater rafting. And in a place of such natural beauty. Amazing. But it also says you and the other kids will be responsible for looking after yourselves. Cooking, cleaning, washing. Reckon you can cope with that? I mean, your mother and I do everything for you here. It's a wonder you manage to wipe your own bum.'

Rose sniggered and kicked me under the table. Mum rose to my defence.

'That's not fair, Michael,' she said.

'You mean he doesn't manage to wipe his own bum?' Dad laughed.

Rose spluttered into her Weet-Bix.

'You are soooo funny, Daddy,' she chortled.

'Marcus can look after himself, can't you dear?' said

Mum. 'He does the dishes twice a week. And remember the time he cooked us a meal on our anniversary?'

'Remember?' said Dad. 'I've been trying to forget. Pasta and custard.'

'I thought that was a cook-in sauce,' I said. Boy, was I never going to be allowed to forget that? Actually, I'd thought it was kinda yummy.

'Anyway,' said Dad. 'It should be the making of you. Like a boot camp. Maybe when you get back you'll keep your bedroom tidy.'

I was going to point out the pigs flying past the window, but decided against it.

'I'll miss you, Marcus,' trilled Rose, her shoe thudding with unerring accuracy into my shin. Mum and Dad smiled at each other. It's possible that cartoon hearts rose up from the table and popped in midair.

*Yeah,* I thought. *My shin is really looking forward to you missing me.*

'I'll miss you too, Rose,' I said.

*Like a poke in the eye with a burnt stick.*


'You're dead meat, Mucus,' said John Oakman as he kicked me in the shin. 'Hey. Geddit? Mucus. Slimy stuff. Your name's Marcus. Mucus. Geddit?'

The school minibus had travelled about two hundred metres on our journey to the ferry. This wasn't the best possible start to the trip.

I rubbed my shin and looked John up and down, which took a bit of time.

The first thing to strike you about John (apart from his

boot into your shin) is his height. You get a crick in your neck just trying to make eye contact. I've known shorter telegraph poles. He's a hazard for low-flying aircraft. Sometimes his head disappears into clouds. Occasionally, his shoulders become crusted with snow.

He's tall, okay?

I considered his friendly attempts to strike up a relationship. Mucus? A kick in the shin? These were the trademarks of Rose, the sister from hell. For a moment, I wondered whether John was Rose in disguise. Perhaps she couldn't bear to be separated from the object of her torture for a week, and had undergone cosmetic surgery to get on this trip. I wouldn't put it past her to have a sex change just to make my life miserable.

Or maybe she'd *possessed* John. Like in those horror flicks when demons take over someone's body, live inside them and force them to commit acts of evil.

Rose was evil enough, and there was enough room inside John. For Rose *and* a couple of mates standing on her shoulders.

Then I thought it through and decided that it was just coincidence. Fortune was pooing in my back pocket again. However, I was going to be spending the next week with John, so I needed to get to know him.

'Why am I dead meat, John?' I asked him in my most reasonable voice. 'I've not done anything to you.'

He mulled this over. John isn't known for the quickness of his mind. Maybe it's something to do with his brain being starved of oxygen at high altitude. If he ever had a thought, it would die of loneliness.

'Have, Mucus,' he said finally. 'You exist. Me don't like it.'

He was about to kick me in the shin again. I could see his brain struggling to send the message to his leg. But it didn't happen, and not just because of the distance the message would have had to travel. Dyl came between us.

'Hey, John,' he said in a friendly voice. 'Just so you know, Marcus is my mate. Anything happens to him and I take it personally. Get my meaning?'

This was very complicated for John, and he took his time processing the information. Finally, comprehension struggled into his eyes.

'Sure, Dyl, mate. Got yer.'

Everyone is scared of Dylan, which makes him a useful friend to have. I really don't know why. He's built like a pencil and isn't much taller. John, on the other hand, is built like a skyscraper. Put them side by side and Dylan wouldn't be able to touch his kneecap. Yet it was obvious who was top dog. Nonetheless, I'd have to keep my eye on John. Not that that was difficult. He dominated the landscape.

John went to the back of the minibus where the rest of the kids were mooning cars on the freeway. I hoped he wasn't going to join in. If he bent over, he'd headbutt our driver.

The bus left us at the ferry terminal. Eight of us, including Mr Crannitch, hoisted our bags on our shoulders and found a fast-food joint. It was six in the evening. The school day had really dragged, especially since I'd spent the recess and lunch breaks locked in a cubicle in the boys' toilets. Tonia Niven just doesn't give up.

The ferry was due to leave at eight. According to Mr Crannitch, another bus would pick us up from East Devonport in Tassie and take us to our destination in the heart of the Tasmanian wilderness. We would meet our guides on this bus – some special dudes with considerable experience of survival techniques and dealing with problem kids. I got the feeling Mr Crannitch was looking forward to that. Like I said, he used to be young and energetic before he came to our school and got saddled with the special boys unit. Now he looked like Yoda with extra wrinkles.

I fronted up to the fast-food counter. A young guy with a face like a pizza chewed gum and stared at me blankly.

'Excuse me,' I said. 'Can you tell me where your meat comes from?'

I'm fussy about the meat I eat. I try to avoid anything that involves cruelty.

'Yeah,' he said.

There was a long silence. I drummed my fingers on the counter. He snapped his gum.

'So where *does* it come from?' I said finally.

'The freezer.'

I tried again.

'Okay. But before the freezer?'

'A delivery truck.'

This was getting me nowhere.

'Any chance of a supervisor?' I asked.

'Just what you see on the menu.'

I sighed. Then I noticed a sign on the menu board. OUR BURGERS ARE MADE FROM 100% PRIME-CUT AUSTRALIAN BEEF. This was encouraging but didn't give enough information.

'Is there cruelty involved when your cows are butchered?' I said.

He looked at me as if I was a moron.

'Well, they're butchered,' he replied. 'I guess the cows reckon that's kinda cruel.'

He was right, of course. I was a moron. But I was also starving, there was nothing vegetarian on the menu and the queue behind me was getting restless. Guilt and hunger battled. Hunger won. I ordered a cheeseburger, a double helping of fries and made a solemn vow this would be the last time my conscience would lose out to my stomach.

After we'd eaten and Mr Crannitch had tried to stop the other boys from seeing how far they could throw French fries, we got on *The Spirit of Tasmania*, a huge boat that would take us across Bass Strait. We filed past a long line of cars waiting to load, presented our tickets to a guy in a booth and made our way up the gangplank and from there to the passenger level. Mr Crannitch held up his hands.

'Now, boys,' he said. 'You are representing our school on this trip and bad behaviour will not be tolerated. If anyone steps out of line ...'

He looked around. Only me and Dylan were still there. The rest had disappeared in a blaze of shouting, screaming and arm-punching.

'... then I will make another idle threat,' he finished.

'Don't worry, sir,' said Dyl. 'I'll make sure they behave.'

Mr Crannitch licked his lips.

'Thanks, Dylan,' he said. 'We are sleeping in the Ocean View Recliners on C Deck. Tell the boys they must be there by ten o'clock. I'm ... I'm just going to explore the boat.'

He hurried off to what looked suspiciously like a bar. Dyl went in search of the others. He's like that, Dyl. If he says he's going to do something, then he will.

So I had the chance to do a little exploring. Most of the ship was taken up with bars and restaurants, though there were plenty of lounges and even an arcade games section. As I passed it I saw all of the special boys in there. Probably a blessing. Everyone's well-behaved in arcades. Put a computer game in front of us and we'll stare at the screen as if hypnotised. Set off dynamite and we won't flinch. I might have gone in myself but I needed fresh air.

Most of the passengers were inside, so the decks were generally empty. As the boat set off, I stood at the very front and felt the cold air blow through my hair. After half an hour or so, I could feel spray against my cheeks. We were picking up speed. Lights twinkled on distant shores. When I looked back I saw Melbourne dwindling into the distance, braceleted with lights like a vast Christmas decoration. There was no one else around and that suited me. The air felt sharp and clean. I could smell the sea.

And something else…

At first, it was faint, a ghost smell. Then it hit me between the eyes and I almost retched.

'For God's sake, Blacky!' I yelled. 'That has to be you. Nothing smells as bad as that. Nothing.'

'You're very kind, mush,' said Blacky's voice in my head. 'I like to think I'm unique.'

I turned and there he was, sitting on a bench. It was lucky no one else was on deck. Otherwise there might have been a major disaster. People throwing themselves overboard to escape the smell. I was tempted myself. When Blacky exudes a particularly foul odour, death loses its sting.

'Phwoah, Blacky,' I said. 'I thought you'd stopped farting! Changed your diet. But that is evil, even by your standards.'

'Thanks, tosh. I aim to please. But I *have* stopped farting.'

'So what's that smell, then? Aftershave?'

'I have rediscovered the joy of rolling in various things I find in the course of my travels. This, for example, is the result of a happy encounter with a small mound of rotting fish guts, seasoned with the merest hint of seagull poop. Stumbled across it on one of the piers. Superlative bouquet.'

'Why do dogs do that, Blacky? Roll in nasty-smelling stuff.'

'Why do humans not?'

I considered asking him to drop his guts, just to mask the ripe aroma that shimmered around him in a haze. I would have thrown him overboard but my eyes were watering so much I couldn't see him properly. At least we weren't inside the boat. If Blacky had been on the *Titanic*, they would have *aimed* for the iceberg.

'I made it, Blacky,' I said, giving up the previous topic of conversation as a bad job. 'On my way to Tassie.'

'You are phenomenally good—'

I blushed.

'—at stating the obvious. But this is the easy bit, tosh. What you must do over the next four or five days will challenge you in ways you've never experienced. It's going to be the toughest thing you've ever done. So I suggest you get a good night's sleep and warn that wazzock Dylan about what's in store.'

*Wazzock?* I had no idea what that was, but I guessed it wasn't a compliment. And how could I warn Dyl about what was in store? I had no idea, because Blacky, the foul, stinking, loathsome mutt, had refused to tell me. An awful thought crossed my mind.

'You're not thinking of bunking down with us tonight, are you, Blacky?'

He snorted.

'In the budget recliners section? I don't think so, bucko. I only travel first class. I have my own cabin. Very comfortable. Very private.'

'And how did you manage that, then? Mastercard?'

'No. The cabin was booked by an elderly American couple. For some reason, they came into the cabin, took a couple

of deep breaths, vomited and left. Strange, that. But I'm not complaining.'

'You're not bothered about sharing your sleeping space with vomit?'

A misty look came into Blacky's eyes.

'Almost irresistible,' he breathed. 'I only hope someone doesn't get in there with a mop, bucket and disinfectant.'

I caught up with Dylan in the games arcade.

I took him to one side and explained that a smelly, off-white dog was on board. I hadn't told him about Blacky's appearance in my bedroom the previous week. It would only have got him worked up. And getting Dyl worked up is about as wise as microwaving a hand grenade.

He was thrilled.

'So what is it, Marc? What's the mission?'

And I was forced to explain that I was more in the dark than a coal miner during a power blackout.

Dyl got the rest of the boys back to the sleeping station by eleven o'clock, only an hour after Mr Crannitch's deadline. Not that it seemed to bother Mr Crannitch. He was snoring loudly in one of the recliner chairs, drool running down his chin.

I think the boys might have just gone straight back to the arcade, but the boat was running into bad weather. For the last half hour, there'd been a distinct swell, and the boat was rocking violently. A few of the boys looked green around the gills. Everyone found a recliner and tried to settle down to sleep. But the pitching and tossing

grew steadily worse. After a while it was obvious I wasn't going to sleep.

I figured it was probably better to get some fresh air. Being in a confined space made my stomach churn. I hadn't eaten since the fast-food place, which was probably good. If the sea got any rougher I'd certainly be seeing my cheeseburger again. With relish.

I lurched from my recliner and headed for the door. As soon as my feet hit the floor I knew I was in trouble. It was the weirdest feeling, as through the world was on springs. I tried to take a step, but the floor moved beneath my feet. I planted one foot firmly and waited while everything tilted and steadied. Then I took another step. At this rate I'd get to the deck sometime after the ship had docked. I was moving like a sumo wrestler in slo-mo. So I went for the scuttle. Stiff-legged, I weaved drunkenly through the recliners.

It was a relief to get on deck, though it was freezing and the spray from the ocean was like a heavy rain. I peered over the edge of the rail, but the sea was shrouded in darkness. I took deep breaths. My stomach was tossing and turning like the dark waters below.

'Crook, mate?'

I turned. Dylan had followed me. He didn't seem bothered by the ship's movement. In fact he looked downright perky. I felt like something Blacky would want to roll in.

I tried to shake my head but decided against it. Too many things were moving already.

'Any ideas about the mission, Marc?' Dyl asked.

I kept my mouth closed. I was afraid that if I opened it something other than words would come pouring out.

'Hey,' Dyl continued. 'What if it's about Tassie devils? How cool would that be? I mean, our first mission was saving God. It would be fantastic if this one was about saving the Devil. 'Course, it could be anything. I hope it's dangerous, though. Like our last mission. That was the best. Nearly got ourselves killed ...'

His voice droned on, but I wasn't paying attention. Something was boiling to the surface and I was sweating, despite the cold, in my attempts to keep it under control. But I knew it was hopeless. It was fast food going down. It was even faster food coming up.

Listen. Here's a tip that might save you considerable grief in the future. If you're going to throw up on a boat, make sure you're at the back. That way, the puke disappears downwind and into the ocean.

All those diced carrots.

Why is it that when you're sick it always comes up as diced carrots? I've never eaten diced carrots in my life, but every time I upchuck there they are. It's one of life's great mysteries.

Anyway, I wasn't at the back of the boat. I was halfway down one side. I tried to be sick over the railing, but the wind caught it and blew it over my right shoulder. Back on board. A thick cloud of hamburger meat and diced carrots.

It would be amusing to tell you that it drenched Dyl, but he was standing in front of me. Upwind. What is less amusing – for me, at least – was that someone else had come on deck without me noticing. John Oakman stood there, his face and hair covered. I watched as he slowly wiped his eyes clear. My stomach lurched again. He was

35

not pleased, which is hardly surprising. But it wasn't just anger reflected in those distant eyes.

It was murder.

I was dead meat. Which was appropriate, since that's what I'd just covered John with.

Along with diced carrots, of course.

Dylan discovered me cowering in a cleaner's cupboard half an hour later. He said he would protect me, but I couldn't sleep in a recliner only a few metres from John. So I found a lounge as far away as possible. The seats were uncomfortable and I was forced to keep an eye on the door in case an evil beanpole smelling of puke entered in search of vengeance.

He didn't.

By the time we docked in East Devonport at seven in the morning I was shattered. The weather had improved and it was cold but clear. Judging by the appearance of the other boys, we were all suffering. I'm not sure which was heavier – the bags on our shoulders or the ones under our eyes.

Mr Crannitch also seemed under the weather as we went down the gangplank. He clutched his head whenever there was a noise. Not even a loud noise. He reacted to normal conversation as though someone was poking him in the eye with a needle.

We were met at the terminal by our guides, instructors

37

from the Wilderness Camp. Two of them. They couldn't have been more different.

One wasn't much taller than me. He had a shaved head and was packed with muscle. I mean his head was packed with muscle. It bulged in strange places. Not that the rest of him was short on power. He wore a tracksuit that strained to keep all of him safely gathered in. It was as if he'd been cling-wrapped. His legs were huge and so bandy he couldn't stop a pig in a corridor. He'd rolled up the sleeves of his tracksuit top, exposing massive forearms folded across a barrel of a chest. I'd never seen such hairy arms. I've stepped on carpets that weren't as thick. He was a pocket King Kong.

The other dude was taller, thinner and, on first impressions at least, friendlier. At least he was smiling, whereas the small gorilla looked as though he was chewing on a lemon. This guy appeared fit and lithe. Judging by his face, he'd spent a lot of time outdoors. His skin was brown, leathery and criss-crossed with lines. The only worry was that he sported a short, braided pigtail. It was as if he had a length of grey rope stapled to the back of his neck.

I don't trust old people with pigtails. They labour under the delusion they're young and listen to the same bands you do. This is unnatural. There should be a law against it.

Anyway, we stood in a ragged line while the bandy-legged chimp paced in front of us, giving us a close examination. He stopped in front of me. His nostrils were like shotgun barrels. I felt as if I was gazing into two large caves. I half expected to see a possum in one.

'Aye, a'reet,' he barked, taking a step back and addressing

all of us. 'Ma name's Jimmeh. This here's ma colleague Phul. Now. Reet. There'll be nae botha oan this camp.' His beady eyes swept over us. His nostrils followed suit. I worried for a moment we might get blasted by both barrels. 'Dinnae think, fir one moment, thit ma arse is made o' mince or thit ma heid buttons up the back. Aye. Reet. Phul.'

He stepped back and flexed his arm muscles. Hairs writhed as if small animals were burrowing under the surface. I gave a sideways glance at the rest of the boys and, judging by their expressions, they were thinking exactly the same. Not only was one of the guys in charge closely related to a Yowie, but he hadn't yet got to grips with the English language. If he was a film, we'd have needed subtitles.

The other dude stepped forward.

'Thanks, Jimmy,' said the Pigtail. 'As you've heard, my name is Phil and we are your guides and instructors on this camp. You will follow us to the bus and stow your luggage. We have a three-hour drive, but we'll stop on the way to pick up provisions and get a bite to eat.'

He pulled at his pigtail and I caught the glint of an earring. It was worse than I'd thought. A pigtail *and* an earring. He'd probably get out a guitar for a singsong around the camp fire and be ripped to pieces by a pack of desperate twelve-year-olds. But at least we could understand what he said.

'This will be your only chance to do essential shopping,' Phil continued. 'Trust me, where we are going there are no corner shops. Any questions? Good. Follow me.'

I particularly liked the way he asked if we had questions and then didn't give us the chance to ask any. Looking

at Jimmy, though, I had the feeling Dad was right. This camp was going to be *tough*. A wiry hippie and a furry, musclebound primate speaking his own private language wasn't the best of starts.

Within five minutes we had our stuff loaded and the bus took off. I was surprised how quickly we left Devonport behind. I sat at the front of the bus behind Mr Crannitch and Phil. Jimmy was driving and occasionally muttering something unintelligible.

It was a good view up front. Plus, I wanted to keep well away from John. Apart from Dyl, the other boys were crowded at the back. There's a scientific law, like gravity, that says boys – especially those with behavioural problems – always sit at the back of anything. Classrooms, buses, the gym during assemblies.

It might have been Einstein who first discovered this.

Mr Crannitch, however, was the first to discover something else. He turned in his seat and crinkled his nose.

'Can anyone smell something nasty?'

There were whoops and cheers from the back of the bus.

'That's John, sir. He's full of crap.'

'Am not!'

'Are too, ya stinkin' mongrel.'

'It's Brodie's armpits, sir.'

'Who's dropped their guts?'

There was plenty more, but I didn't follow any of it. Maybe I've become conditioned, but whenever there's an inexplicable bad smell I always jump to one conclusion.

I didn't have to wait long to receive confirmation.

'Cat poo,' announced Blacky's voice in my head. 'With

a soupçon of well-digested furball marinated in urine. Top-quality odour.'

'Where are you, Blacky?'

'In the luggage hold, tosh. See how considerate I am? I could have hopped on board with the rest of you. You know I am a master of disguise and can infiltrate anywhere.'

I sighed. Judging by the smell, which was really starting to get a hold, I suppose we should have been counting our blessings.

I could see Jimmy's nostrils flexing in the rear-view mirror. Given their size, he must have been copping it worse than the rest of us. Phil went around and opened windows. A cold breeze flooded the bus, but it was better than the alternative.

I glanced at my watch. There was a long trip ahead. Maybe this was a good opportunity to get the lowdown on the mission that Blacky had promised before we set off. I reminded myself, however, that Blacky's promises normally don't amount to much. This time, to my surprise, he kept his word.

'What do you know about the thylacine, tosh?' he said.

'Is it a painkiller?' I replied.

He snorted.

'Modelling putty?' I tried.

'Slap me in the belly with a wet fish,' he said. 'I despair of modern education. Kids today. You probably think a one-man sub is a large sandwich.'

'You mean it isn't?'

'How about the Tasmanian tiger, mush? Does that ring bells?'

It did. I'd done an oral once on endangered species, and I'd looked up the Tasmanian tiger on the internet.

'It's extinct, Blacky. The last one died in … the 1930s, I think.'

'The last captive Tasmanian tiger died at Hobart Zoo in 1936. Quite right. But the thylacine, to give it its proper name, was only officially declared extinct in 1986. It would be an unlikely coincidence indeed for a captive animal to be the last remaining specimen.'

'But no one's seen a Tassie tiger for over seventy years.'

'Wrong, tosh. Quite wrong. Why does that not surprise me? There have been hundreds of sightings of the Tassie tiger. What you mean is that no scientist has captured one and been able to prove beyond a shadow of a doubt that it exists, which is probably very good news for the tiger.'

I was starting to get excited. I could see where this was leading.

'You mean there *are* tigers out there, Blacky? It's not extinct after all?'

There was a long silence.

'Do you know why the thylacine, once plentiful in Tasmania, became endangered, tosh?'

I'd done enough reading to know the answer to that one. Human behaviour. It always has been and always will be, unless we do something really, really soon to change our ways. It is the main reason why Australia has the worst record of any continent for loss of species. Nearly half of all Australian mammals have become extinct in the last two hundred years. It is astonishing until you realise that two hundred years is precisely how long white settlers

43

have been on the land. I can never think of this without tears coming to my eyes.

'Destruction of the environment, Blacky,' I said. 'Land clearing, wiping out habitats.'

'You're learning, mush. Very good. But in the case of the Tassie tiger, humanity took a more hands-on approach in addition to all that. In the late 1800s the tiger was so plentiful that the government believed it was responsible for killing sheep and chickens introduced by settlers – *introduced*, note. It decided to offer a bounty, a reward for killing them. A pound in the old currency – a lot of money in those days – for each skin. Hunters and farmers slaughtered as many as they could. And do you know the really funny thing, tosh?'

I didn't. And I had a feeling it wasn't going to be funny at all.

'The tiger wasn't responsible for the vast majority of the attacks. That was feral dogs, with a little input from the Tasmanian *devil*. Yet the thylacine was slaughtered to the point of extinction. How do you like that?'

I didn't. I didn't like that at all.

'You haven't answered my question, Blacky,' I said. 'There *are* tigers still out there. I'm right, aren't I?'

The silence was even longer this time.

'You might be, mush. But you need to know one thing. If there are tigers still out there, their fate is entirely in your hands.'

I spent the rest of the journey looking out of the window. I suppose, living in a city, I'd become used to shopping centres, roads and housing estates that stretched to the horizon. Tasmania isn't like that at all.

Most of the time we travelled on empty roads, every so often passing through a small town. It was the number of trees that surprised me. They were everywhere. And we seemed to be moving deeper and deeper into vast forest.

Just after ten o'clock we stopped at a small town in the middle of nowhere. Phil produced an esky full of sandwiches and cold drinks and we ate in a park under the shade of a tree. After that, we hit the tiny supermarket to stock up on rations. I bought chocolate. Mum had already looked after the whole toothpaste and shower gel department, so I just had to consider my stomach. I took the opportunity to have a word with Phil about food on the camp itself. If necessary I'd buy my own vegie burgers. It turned out he

was a vegetarian and he assured me there were sufficient supplies for both of us.

Dylan bought two cartons of cola. He'd have bought more, but Jimmy wouldn't let him stow them into the luggage hold. He barked something in his foreign language and Phil translated.

Incidentally, there was no sign of a small, dirty-white and smelly hound in the bowels of the hold. Bowels was probably the right word. It *stank* in there.

Dyl was worried. He tried to do the maths, but that's never been one of his strong points.

'Seven days, two cartons of cola each with twenty-four cans. That's how many cans, Marc?'

'Forty-eight.'

'Seven goes into forty-eight how many times?'

'That's seven cans a day, Dyl.' I didn't mention that this would give him one day with only six. It was another need-to-know thing.

'WHAAAT? Seven! I can't exist on seven. I have seven cans before breakfast.'

'Dyl, you have seven cans *instead* of breakfast,' I pointed out.

'Oh, man.'

I tried to take his mind off this catastrophe by filling him in on what Blacky had told me. He perked up immediately. That's a good thing about Dyl's short-term memory problem. You could tell him that he was two minutes away from being run over by a Mack truck, change the subject and he'd be as happy as Larry.

By the way, I've always wanted to meet someone called

Larry, just to see if he is constantly laughing.

'Cool, Marc. A tiger, huh? Huge thing, slashing jaws, claws that can rip you apart. Fantastic.'

'It's more like a medium-sized dog, Dyl,' I said. 'In fact, it's a marsupial.'

Dyl looked baffled, so I explained. 'It has a pouch for its young. The reason it's called a tiger is that it has stripes over its body, particularly towards the tail.'

'And everyone reckons there aren't any left?'

I nodded.

'It would be so cool if we got to see one, hey?'

Having successfully distracted his mind from the cola crisis, I got back on the bus. John gave me a vicious kick in the shin as he shimmied past.

'Sorry, Mucus,' he growled. 'Accident.'

The last forty-five minutes of our trip was down a dirt road into a huge forest. Occasionally, I would catch a glimpse of a river sparkling off to one side, but then the trees would sweep in again and block the view. It was cold. Mr Crannitch had shut the windows after our last stop, but even so Jimmy had been forced to put the heating on. And *he* was insulated by half a metre of thick hair.

It was eleven in the morning. I hated to think what the temperature would be like at night.

Finally, we came to a stop at a large gate that blocked the road. There was a sign on it that read, PRIVATE PROPERTY. THE WILDERNESS LODGE RETREAT. NO UNAUTHORISED ENTRY. Phil hopped off the bus, unlocked the padlock on the gate and we drove through. Jimmy didn't bother to

wait for his mate, but swung the bus around a bend into a large clearing and cut the engine.

We were here. Wherever 'here' was.

I jumped down from the bus. It was good to stretch my legs after so long. The biggest building in the clearing was a log cabin off to my right. Well, I say cabin, but it was more the size of a single-storey house. A few other, smaller, cabins were dotted around. I instantly deduced that one of them was a shower room and toilet block. You can put this down to the fact that I'm a gifted detective. Mind you, a big sign saying SHOWER ROOM AND TOILET BLOCK gave me a slight clue. On the other side of the dirt track where the bus was parked was a wooden-framed barbecue area. The air was so cold I could see my breath.

Thank goodness Mum had insisted on packing thermal underwear. I'd thrown a huge hissy fit when she suggested it. I swore I would sooner have my teeth torn out with red-hot pliers than wear them. Pack my jocks with ice and I'd still not wear them. She'd ignored me, though.

We all got off the bus and the two instructors opened the luggage compartment. Phil pointed to the large building.

'Your dorm,' he said. 'Twenty bunks, so there's plenty of room. Get your luggage, make yourselves at home and we'll see you out here in fifteen minutes. Sharp, guys.'

I was relieved it wasn't Jimmy giving the instructions. We'd still be there scratching our heads.

The dorm was basic and you could smell years of sweat soaked into the woodwork. But at least it had a wood-burning stove. Unlit at the moment. I waited until John chose his bunk before putting my stuff on the one furthest

48

away. It was going to be difficult enough getting to sleep as it was. I hoped that if John did try to make a night-time visit to my bunk I'd hear the groan of shifting floorboards. Or his head scraping against the ceiling. Even then I could have done with additional resources. Like a moat. Or a missile launcher. Maybe both.

Phil and Jimmy were pacing up and down when we reassembled outside twenty minutes later. My impression was that Jimmy, in particular, never relaxed. Probably went swinging through trees while everyone else slept. He took a pace forward. His eyes bulged and his face was red. It looked like a relief map of Mars.

'Fifteen!' he yelled. 'Ya barkin' wee minkers. Ya bahmpots. Ya choobs. Awa' and boil yir heids.'

Phil stepped in.

'Jimmy's right, guys,' he said. No one argued with this, for the very good reason we had no idea what Jimmy had just said. 'When we say fifteen minutes, we mean fifteen. Not twenty. Not thirty. Fifteen. Got it? Okay.'

He put his hands behind his back. 'Here's the plan for today. We are going to start with a simple team-building exercise. After lunch, we'll take a small hike into the bush. No more than two kilometres. This will be preparation for a longer hike we'll take the day after tomorrow. When we return, depending on time, we might take the kayaks out onto the river.'

I put my hand up. Phil nodded at me.

'Won't it be cold in the water?' I asked. The temperature had dropped even further. A penguin would have been on the lookout for a fleecy jumper and a hot-water bottle.

'And?' said Phil.

'I was wondering if there was heating in the kayaks?'

Phil laughed, but Jimmy appeared to get even redder. I worried the top of his head might explode. He took a couple of paces forward, elbowing Phil out of the way. He turned the twin bores of his nostrils towards me.

'Heat, is it?' he yelled. 'I'll give ya heat, lad. Do ye know why yir kayak wud freeze the wee bits oaf a brass monkey?'

At least I understood most of this. It seemed like progress.

'No,' I said.

'Because ye cannae huv yir kayak an' heat it,' he said. Then he burst out laughing. 'Geddit?' he spluttered. 'Yir kayak an' heat it. Tha's a wee cracker, so it is.'

Phil stepped in once again.

'After that,' he said, ignoring his colleague, who appeared to be on the verge of suffocating on his own laughter, 'you'll be preparing the evening meal – a barbecue – and cleaning up afterwards. Bed will be at eight-thirty, ready for a six o'clock warm-up run in the morning. Any questions?'

This time he did pause, but no one said anything. I think we were too stunned. I'd been hoping for an opportunity to read a book, maybe catch a quick afternoon nap. Possibly a swim in the resort pool, some television in the games room, a leisurely buffet dinner before settling down in front of a new-release DVD on a forty-two-inch plasma screen. That's my idea of doing it tough. Unfortunately, we appeared to be lacking a few of the essentials. Like a pool, a games room and a television.

We trailed after our guides as they led us down to the banks of a slow-moving river. It wasn't a big river, maybe twelve metres across, but it looked cold. I half expected to see the odd iceberg floating past. Or even a normal iceberg.

Jimmy still hadn't recovered from his own wit, so Phil gave us instructions.

'Your task is to construct a way of getting across this river. Three rules. One, the members of your team must all travel together. You can't go one by one. Two, the only tools you have are a length of rope and a small machete. Three, you cannot cut anything down from the forest. Anything you use must already be lying around. Two teams. Start when you're ready.'

Dyl and I were on the same team. Unfortunately, the other two members were John and Kyle. Kyle had a face like roadkill, a home-pierced eyebrow and the attention span of a goldfish. He didn't fill me with confidence. We got into a huddle, which was a good idea since we exchanged heat. I was starting to lose feeling in my extremities. Unfortunately, we were also exchanging body odours. Kyle was part fish. Fish that had been left out in the sun for a couple of days. I broke away.

'Any ideas?' I asked.

The signs weren't good. Kyle shuffled songs on his iPod and Dyl drained his fifth cola of the day. At this rate he'd run out by the weekend. John, meanwhile, did a stunning impersonation of a tree. Time for Marcus to take charge.

I had two ideas. The first was to spread John across the river and use him as a bridge. I didn't suggest it. The second involved building a raft.

'C'mon guys,' I said. 'We need to work together here. There's no I in team.'

'No Z either,' said John. 'What's your point?'

'There *is* a B in banana, though,' chipped in Kyle. 'Isn't there?'

'And plenty of As,' said Dyl. 'Why? Has anyone got a banana? I'm starving.'

I sighed.

'Forget the bananas,' I said. 'We need to build a raft.'

'Hate fruit,' said John. 'Not a monkey. Need Mars bar.'

It took some time to get the subject away from food, but eventually we fanned out along the bank of the river and collected logs and fallen branches. I kept a firm hold on the machete. I didn't trust John.

The other team were also collecting wood, but I got the impression they were just copying us. We dragged the bigger branches down to the riverbank. The key, I reckoned, was speed. We didn't need to build a catamaran with carved figurehead, sundeck and tennis court. Just a bog-standard raft, big enough to take the weight of three boys and a human giraffe.

I selected eight branches and lopped off unnecessary foliage. Dyl and John took each branch as I finished it and lashed them together with rope. Kyle scrolled through his iPod.

John surprised me. He knew what he was doing with the rope, first of all dunking it into the river and then weaving it through the individual branches. Finally, he tightened the whole structure with a slipknot.

'Rope wet,' he said. 'Tightens when dry.'

'Cool, John,' I said. I felt brown-nosing wouldn't hurt. 'Were you in the Cub Scouts?'

John snorted.

'Nah, Mucus,' he replied. 'Executioner. Career aim. Read a book once.' I tried to keep the surprise out of my face. I'd have put money on John being incapable of colouring in a book, let alone reading one. 'Knots. Need knots to hang people.'

It wasn't the right time to point out that we don't have capital punishment in Australia anymore. It's not a good idea to upset a potential homicidal maniac.

Both groups finished their rafts at the same time. It wasn't fair. The other group had just imitated us, move for move. But I had a secret weapon. True, I was banking on the other kids being idiots, but nothing I'd seen so far suggested I might be mistaken. As soon as our misshapen raft was finished, I jumped about like a frog on a sugar rush.

'Hurry, guys,' I yelled. 'Get this in the water. We can't let them win.'

It was a simple plan, but it worked. The other group grabbed their raft, flung it onto the slow-moving waters of the river and leaped on board. The whole contraption rocked violently, threatening to send the boys into the water. Then it settled. I had my hand on the edge of our raft, stopping it from being launched. I wanted to see if I was right.

I was. The other group panicked for a moment, shuffled to get their balance. Then, when they saw they were safely floating and we weren't even on the water, their expressions turned to glee.

'Ha! Losers.'

'Eat my shorts!'

One of the boys dropped his dacks to moon us, but the

movement caused the raft to wobble alarmingly. The rest of his group grabbed and steadied him.

'C'mon, Marc,' said Dyl. 'They're going to beat us.'

'No, they're not,' I said. 'Watch.'

I loved the way the expressions of the boys on the raft changed from triumph to despair. They had forgotten one thing. Adrift on the river, they had no way of steering. The current caught their raft and took it gently downriver. The other bank was only ten metres away, but it might as well have been ten kilometres. They drifted off into the distance.

I held up the long poles I had been saving as a way of pushing us across the river. We could have used John for the same purpose, but I figured he might resent it.

'Wave goodbye, guys,' I said.

The four of us waved at the dwindling raft in the centre of the river. One of the other group even waved back.

'Bon voyage,' I yelled. 'Send us a postcard.'

After that, it was simple. We stepped carefully onto our raft, making sure it wasn't going to capsize. I handed one pole to John and kept the other. Then we carefully punted our way across. When we landed on the opposite bank we'd only moved a few metres downriver. One by one, we stepped onto land.

'Yay! We won.'

There was jubilation. We punched the air. We gave each other high-fives. We slapped each other on the back. I gave John Oakman a playful thump between the shoulder-blades.

We were tight. We were pals. We'd bonded as a group.

Unfortunately, as my hand made contact with John's back, he stood on a slippery stone. His foot slid. And then it was like one of those old films I'd seen of tall trees being felled. I was tempted to yell TIMBERRRR! I didn't.

I watched as he fell into the icy cold water.

I watched as he got to his feet, dripping wet and starting to shiver.

I watched as he turned to glare at me.

We were loose. We were un-pals. We'd come unstuck.

Oops.

It was evening and colder than a polar bear's armpit.

We hadn't got the kayaks out, though we *had* gone on a two-kilometre hike into the bush. There hadn't been time for everything. Firstly, the other group had to be rescued. Jimmy and Phil threw them a rope and towed them to shore. Pity in a way. I'd kinda been hoping for a waterfall. Then we defrosted John. He looked like an icy pole. I reckon it was the only thing that saved me. He'd have killed me if he hadn't been frozen to the ground. I thought it was good odds we'd have to take a blowtorch to him. We didn't. Instead, our guides built a small fire, then wrapped him in blankets and stuck him in front of it. I was going to suggest putting up a couple of split sticks over the fire and turn him on it like a spit, but kept the idea to myself.

Now we were all wrapped in our warmest clothes and huddled around a huge open fire. Overhead, the sky was packed tight with hard, bright stars.

'Reet, ye big jessies, ya wee girls' blouses,' yelled Jimmy. He appeared to have got his volume control stuck. Whatever

he said – and none of us could understand much anyway – was said at maximum decibel count. 'Nae carry-oot here. Ye want tae eat, ye cook yersen.'

'Time to get the barbecue going,' added Phil. I think he realised he was also translator.

'Phil?' I said, as we put kindling under the barbecue grill and Jimmy lugged out a big esky with meat in it.

'Yeah, mate?'

'Where is Jimmy from?'

Phil smiled and tugged at his earring.

'Having trouble with the accent? Scotland, mate. Glasgow, originally.'

'So he's only just come to Australia?'

'Been here thirty years.'

I was amazed.

'Then why hasn't he learned the language?'

Phil laughed.

'They speak English in Scotland, mate,' he said. 'Just not as we know it. If you think this is bad, you should have heard him thirty years ago. Compared to that, he's positively ocker now.'

'He called us jessies and big girls' blouses. What's that mean?'

'Sooks. But don't mind Jimmy. He insults everyone. It's just the way he is. But he *is* tough. Ex SAS. Hard as nails. For all that, he's one of the kindest people I've ever known. A top bloke. Now, mate. To quote Jimmy, quit bumpin' yer gums – stop chatting – and help get the barbie ready.'

There were snags. There were fat steaks. There were onions. And, for Phil and me, there were vegie burgers.

Once the hotplate was sizzling, we slapped on the food and the delicious smell of barbecuing filled the clearing. I was impressed. I didn't know about the other kids in the special boys unit, but I did know Dyl and me. Give us two bits of bread and a slice of cheese and we'd have struggled to make a sandwich. But here we were, getting up a hearty feed for ten.

'Make that eleven, mush,' came a voice in my head.

I paused in my stirring of the fried onions.

'Blacky!' I said silently. 'I was worried. Where are you?'

I'd heard nothing from the grumpy hound since early that morning. He'd kept a low profile. It was so cold I was concerned for his safety. It's not like he's got a thick coat. I'd pictured him somewhere out in the bush, half-frozen, half-starving. Huddled under a tree, keeping warm by burrowing under fallen leaves. This was hostile territory. And he's not a big dog. I almost got a tear in my eye thinking about it.

'You can save your sympathy, bucko,' said Blacky. 'I've commandeered one of those empty huts as my headquarters. I'm already planning the next stage of the mission.'

Okay. Forget the huddling under a tree. But it was still freezing, even inside our dormitory.

'You must be cold, though, Blacky.'

'I also commandeered a sleeping-bag from the stores. Two, actually. Down-filled. The finest the military makes. If anything, mush, I'm *too* warm.'

My concern was dwindling. From the sound of it, he was much more comfortable than me. Then I thought about food. That must be a problem. I mean, it's not as if he was able to bring an esky with him.

'But you're starving, right?' I asked.

'Not exactly *starving*, tosh. I also commandeered a couple of kilos of dried beef.'

I started to stir the onions again. Here I was, worried about the foul-smelling mutt, and he was living in the lap of luxury. For all I knew, he'd *commandeered* cable TV, a heated indoor swimming pool and a laptop with high-speed internet connection. I had visions of a butler bringing him a cooked breakfast and the morning newspaper while someone else gave him a pedicure.

'Well, you can forget sharing *our* food, Blacky,' I said. 'By the sound of it, you're roughing it in five-star conditions.'

'Be fair, mush. I *am* the brains of this operation. And all I'm asking is a bit of warm food.'

I sighed. 'All right, Blacky, I'll see what I can do.'

'With onions, but no sauce. Make it two snags. Oh, and a steak. Medium rare.'

'Absolutely, sir,' I said. 'Can we interest you in an entree? Wine list? And what about hearing our specials tonight?'

'Oi, tosh,' said Blacky in an offended tone. 'There's no need for sarcasm.' There was a pause. 'Do you *have* any entrees?'

Dinner was a great success, despite the fact that we burned nearly everything. It wasn't so much meat and vegie burgers as charcoal. But everyone was starving and we ate the lot. I stashed a couple of sausages and a particularly incinerated steak in my jacket pocket. Knowing Blacky, he'd send it back and ask for a refund on his bill.

Stuff him.

After we'd cleared up, we gathered around the camp

fire. Although it was freezing, cooking had kept us warm. Now we made a circle around the fire. Phil had brewed a huge billy of tea. Jimmy produced marshmallows and some long skewers. We sat and drank tea and stuffed scorched marshmallows into our faces. It was great. There were only a couple of worries.

One was Mr Crannitch. We hadn't seen him all day, though he'd joined us for dinner. I think he was still sick. From the way he clutched his head, I guess he must have had a headache. He kept sipping from a small metal flask. Painkiller, probably. From time to time he sang a little song to himself. And groaned.

The other worry was John Oakman. He sat opposite me. Whenever I caught his eye, it was clear he wasn't thinking of signing up as the first member of the Marcus Hill fan club. I remembered his ambition of becoming an executioner. John kept looking at my neck. His hands moved as if practising the tying of complicated knots. The marshmallow tasted like ashes in my mouth. Then I realised it *was* ashes. I'd cooked it too long.

'Enjoy it weel ye can,' shouted Jimmy. 'Ah dinnae ken when youse'll get the like agin.'

Maybe I *was* getting used to him. I understood almost all of that.

'Jimmy. Phil,' I said. 'Do you guys think the Tassie tiger still exists?'

This was a good opportunity to do research. Blacky knew a lot, but these guys lived here in Tassie. It seemed sensible to tap into local knowledge.

Jimmy gazed at me over the fire. The flames highlighted

the crags in his skin and threw the bulges in his head into relief. His face writhed in shadow and light.

'Ah'm no the expert oan that,' he bellowed. 'Phul's yir man, there, so he is.'

I turned to Phil. He had his head down. Thinking. Finally, he looked up.

'I *know* they're out there, mate,' he said quietly. 'I've seen one.'

He told his story. It had happened a couple of years ago. He was hiking alone in the forest, about five kilometres from where we were now. He'd turned a corner of the trail and seen it, not ten metres away. The peculiar stiff-legged walk, the strange way the tail stuck out, the stripes. And then it was gone, a blur into the bush. He saw it for less than five seconds. But there was no doubt in his mind what he had seen. A tiger.

'Aye, an' then yir arse fell oaf,' said Jimmy. 'It were a dog, ya dunderheid.'

Phil smiled sadly.

'Jimmy's never believed it, but I know what I saw.' He drained the remains of his tea. 'And it's funny you should mention it, because there's been another sighting recently. Not too far from here. Have you not read about it in the newspapers?'

I shook my head.

'Someone took a photograph, though it was blurred. What you can see is something that *might* be a Tasmanian tiger. Or, as Jimmy would have it, a dog. But everyone's excited. Amateur tiger hunters have come out of the woodwork. Hordes of the buggers, with fancy cameras and night-vision goggles and motion detectors and whatnot. No scientists. They're convinced the tiger has gone. But the romantics are desperate to prove them wrong.'

'What, they're around here?' I asked.

'Mate, you can't throw a rock without hitting one. They're camped about ten kilometres away, which is where the photograph was taken.'

Jimmy snorted.

'Buncha mad rocket mental numpties,' he snarled. 'Ah tell ye, ah hope that critta *is* extinct. 'Cause if them muppets gitta haud of it, it'll be the worse thing that ever happened tae it, so it will.'

I didn't feel qualified to argue with him. Partly because I only understood fifty per cent of what he said.

I was improving. Earlier in the day it had been less than ten per cent.

Mum once said that exercise and fresh air was tiring but gave you a healthy glow. I hadn't listened, mainly because it was *exactly* the thing that old people always said. Like watching television would give you square eyes, carrots helped your eyesight and eating Brussels sprouts was generally a good idea.

But I had never felt so tired in all my life. And it wasn't just because I'd spent a sleepless night manufacturing diced carrots. Judging by the amount I scattered over Bass Strait and John Oakman's face, I should be able to spot a pimple on a mosquito's bum from four kilometres away. My muscles ached and I could barely keep my eyes open. Looking around the camp fire I saw the other kids were

feeling the same. Everyone was yawning, faces were glowing and it wasn't even eight-thirty.

It had to be exercise and fresh air. I wasn't going to tell Mum she was right, though. She'd probably use the admission to push her viewpoint on Brussels sprouts.

'Time to hit the sack, guys,' said Phil. 'And no talking or reading or playing on hand-held game consoles. We're up at sparrow's fart and judging by the look of yous, you all need your beauty sleep.'

We trudged off to the toilet and shower block. All of us except for Kyle, which helped explain the odour of week-old salmon hanging around him in a visible cloud. I hoped someone had brought clothes pegs to put on our noses, otherwise we could all be gassed to death in the middle of the night.

I was first out of the shower. The snags and steak were spreading a grease patch in my jacket pocket. I ducked behind the shower block and called out in my head.

'Blacky? Dinner is served.'

'On my way, mush,' came the reply.

Actually, he could have saved his mental breath. I knew he was close. And not because me and Blacky had bonded. Not because we were like twins and could sense each other's presence.

It was the smell.

Something evil was headed towards me.

'What have you rolled in now, Blacky?' I sighed.

'It's a beauty, isn't it?' said Blacky. He loomed out of the darkness and sat at my feet. 'Stroke of luck, that. Stumbled across a mound of horse poo in the bush. No idea why a

pony would have been out here in the wilderness, but I'm not one to look a gift horse in the mouth. Or the bum, in this case. The mound was old – nicely crisp on the surface but with a very satisfying soft centre once you'd broken through—'

'Yeah, okay,' I interrupted. 'I'd love to share your all-time-favourite top-ten stinks of the decade, but I'm gagging here.' Sniffing Kyle's armpits would have been heaven in comparison. 'Here's your food.'

I put the blackened meat on the ground. Blacky nosed it, then cocked his head and stared at me.

'What's this, ya twonk?' he said. 'Charcoal briquettes from the barbie?'

'The meat's slightly overdone,' I admitted.

'Slightly overdone, mush? *Slightly*? It's buggered. It's blacker than a baboon's bumhole and about as appetising. The secret of good cuisine, bucko, is—'

'Look. Don't eat it, okay. I really don't care. Next time, *you* can do the cooking. *I'll* be the food critic.'

Blacky wolfed the steak. The sausages didn't touch the sides of his throat. I tapped my foot.

'Couldn't have been that bad,' I said.

'It was,' said Blacky. 'It was worse. I just didn't want any other animal eating it. I have, as you know, tosh, a solemn duty to protect all living things, even at the expense of my own wellbeing.'

I turned to go.

'Be ready, mush,' came the voice in my head. 'The mission starts soon.'

'When?'

'In two days. I have an errand to do tomorrow and I'll be back late. I'll give you and Dylan instructions then. But you are going to have to lose the rest of the people here and come with me into the bush. You might want to start thinking about how to do that.'

Losing eight people? I would have welcomed advice, but Blacky had gone. The smell of horse manure lingered a while longer, but soon that was gone too.

I turned towards the dorm.

John Oakman grabbed me as soon as I came around the corner of the shower block. He shoved my arm up my back and pushed me against a tree. I whipped my head about in desperation, but Dyl was nowhere to be seen.

'Puke on me, eh?' snarled John. 'Push me into frozen water, eh? Think you're tough, eh? Think you're hard, eh? Wanna fight, eh?'

'N–no,' I stammered. I was tempted to add 'eh' but didn't. 'Accidents, John. I…I didn't mean to do all that. I'm sorry. I'm really sorry.'

I was hoping that a handsome, frank and open apology would touch his heart. That his eyes would soften, he'd shake my hand, slap me gently on the back and invite me to a sleepover at his place when we got home.

Instead, his eyes narrowed. At least I think they narrowed. It was difficult to tell on account of it being dark. Plus his eyes were about four metres above my head. Maybe if I'd eaten more carrots in my life I could have said for certain.

'C'mon, Mucus,' he said. 'Fight.' His voice took on a mocking tone. 'Or you scared?'

'Me?' I snorted. 'Scared? Me? Scared?' I was playing for time. I considered going for another few repetitions of 'Me? Scared?' in the hope that Dyl would make an appearance, but I didn't think John would fall for it. 'I don't think so,' I added. '*Terrified* would be a much better word. Scared doesn't come close. I'm petrified. I'm quaking in my boots. Well, I would be if I was wearing any. I'm on the point of pooping myself in terror.'

There was silence for a moment way above me.

'You're a sook, Mucus.'

'Absolutely correct, John. Well spotted.'

'Yellow streak. Metre wide.'

'Wider, I think you'll find, John.'

'Not gonna fight, eh?'

I sighed. I thought we'd already established this. For one thing, I'd have needed a ladder just to get close to punching him in the face. And, anyway, I knew how a fight would go. I'd hurl my face into his knuckles, smack my stomach hard into his fist and possibly spread my nose over his forehead.

It's an unorthodox fighting strategy, but one I'd discovered I was good at during the only fight I've ever had.

'No,' I said. 'But thanks for the offer.'

John bent down to look me in the eyes, which was decent of him under the circumstances.

'Gonna get you, Mucus. Bet on it. Sometime. Watch your back.'

And then he uncurled and headed off to the dorm. I followed.

In my experience, being threatened with senseless violence doesn't do wonders for a peaceful night's sleep.

But I was unconscious about ten seconds after my head hit the pillow.

It's that old exercise and fresh air thing again.

Though, between Kyle and Blacky, the air was getting less fresh by the second.

'Aye, a'reet,' bellowed Jimmy. 'Ye cannae sleep yir brains to train oil, ya balloons. Rise and shine and quit yir greetin'.'

The gibberish soaked into my brain and dragged me reluctantly to consciousness. I glanced at my watch. It was five-thirty. Was the dorm on fire? Was there some emergency that would explain why a short, hairy-limbed, bald-headed madman was yelling garbage at us in the middle of the night? I struggled up in bed and tried to peel the sleep from my eyes. Maybe it was a nightmare.

It was, but unfortunately it was a waking one. Jimmy paced up and down. Even in the darkness I could see his face, as red as a traffic light. From all around came groans and mumbles as seven kids reluctantly greeted a new day.

'Fifteen minutes,' roared Jimmy. I was grateful he'd switched to English. 'Ootside by then or ye'll be daein' push-ups.'

This time we were punctual. The general feeling was that Jimmy didn't bluff.

We huddled together in the dark. Seven miserable, freezing kids and two perky instructors.

Listen, if it's okay with you I'll draw a veil over the next couple of hours. There were warming-up exercises, a jog for a couple of kilometres and a final sprint. I hadn't had so much fun since I trod on a rusty nail when I was six and had to have tetanus jabs.

Breakfast was good, though. Jimmy cooked while the rest of us lay gasping on the ground. He did pancakes on the barbie griddle and I'd never tasted anything so excellent in my life. I ate six, smothered in maple syrup. I was hungrier than an overweight hippopotamus on a calorie-controlled diet.

Fresh air and exercise. I tell you. I'd probably have munched through a bucket of Brussels sprouts, though I'd be grateful if you didn't let my mum know that.

After breakfast, we showered and then met up with the instructors in one of the huts. It had been set out like a classroom, with rows of chairs and a whiteboard. There was no sign of Mr Crannitch. I thought it was unfair that *he* could have a lie-in, until I remembered he'd been sick since almost the start of this camp. He must've needed the rest.

Phil did the talking.

'Okay, guys,' he said, pulling at his earring. 'Today is basic survival skills. And putting up tents. Tomorrow, very early, we are hiking in the bush.' He pulled down a map from above the whiteboard. It didn't help much. Trees, more trees, the occasional lake and a crosshatch of dotted lines that appeared to be walking tracks. Phil took out a pointer.

'We will be trekking along this path,' he said. 'Eventually,

we will arrive here.' He smacked the pointer on a small lake. 'Doesn't look far, does it?' We would have nodded but we were too tired and full of pancakes to have the energy. 'In fact, it's a two-day hike. Which means we will be camping along the way. Two people to a tent, so I suggest you find a partner who doesn't mind that you fart, snore and dribble in your sleep.'

I tapped Dyl on the arm. I didn't want to get lumbered with John Oakman, who would probably not only resent my farting, snoring and dribbling but also take issue with my breathing. Dyl nodded. We'd shared a bedroom before.

'Okay,' said Phil. 'We provide tents, sleeping-bags, hiking boots and wet weather gear. What we *don't* provide is their transport. You will carry everything in backpacks. Nor do we help get the tents up. And if any of you are hoping we'll tuck you into your sleeping-bags, check the corners of your tents for monsters and tell you amusing bedtime stories, then I'm afraid you'll be disappointed. Right, all outside and we'll show you how to get the tents assembled.'

It turned out that Kyle was the one who didn't get a partner. Everyone had obviously come to the conclusion that sharing with him would be like bunking down in a rubbish bin with a skunk. So he had to put his tent up by himself, whereas the rest of us at least could work it out in pairs.

It wasn't difficult. The tents were tiny. Me and Dyl are both shorter than average, but it would be tight in there regardless. I wondered how John would fare. He'd have to curl up like a sausage or his legs would stick out the flaps. Wake up and find some critter had eaten them in the night. Mind you, he'd still be taller than me. Maybe in an emergency his partner could use him as a tent pole.

Jimmy and Phil made us put up and take down our tents at least ten times.

'Ye cannae afford tae think aboot it,' Jimmy shouted. 'Oot there, yous'll be caud, wet and buggered wi' tiredness. Ye huv tae dae it oan autopilot.'

Putting up and taking down a tent again and again is not my idea of quality relaxation time, but it gave me the chance to have a private word with Dyl.

I told him what Blacky had said the previous night. Dyl's eyes lit up.

'Cool, Marc. I can't wait. You and me. Another adventure.'

It's a funny thing. I'm the one who is *forced* to go on these adventures. It's only me who can communicate with Blacky, after all. Yet I prefer a quiet life. Don't get me wrong. I *want* to change things for the better. It's just that I'd prefer to do that without running the risk of being eaten or put in jail or becoming lost in a harsh wilderness. Dyl, on the other hand, can't stand the quiet life. He craves excitement. He's in love with danger. Getting eaten or going to jail or being stranded in woop woop holds no terrors for him.

Not for the first time, I thought how lucky I was to have him along.

'Any idea on how we can lose the rest of the group, Dyl?' I asked.

He scrunched up his forehead in thought.

'Nah,' he said. 'Don't worry. We'll work something out when the time comes.'

I glanced around at the rest of the special boys unit. They were working hard at getting the tents up. Phil and Jimmy

73

moved among them, offering encouragement. Something struck me then. Something I'd noticed but hadn't quite got round to thinking about.

'Dyl?' I said. 'What is it with these kids? At school, they are mongrels. They destroy stuff. They swear. You couldn't keep them in a classroom if you padlocked it. Yet, on this camp – so far, at least – they haven't caused any problems. Why's that?'

Dyl looked at me.

'You can't work that one out for yourself?' he said.

I shook my head.

Dyl grinned. 'I thought *you* were the smart one, Marc. They call us "the special boys unit" or "the behaviourally challenged group". Stuff like that. But we know what they really mean. We're the retards, the dropkicks. Thing is, school doesn't suit us. Try to get us in rows, sitting there all quiet while some dude bores us with Maths or reading a dumb book written by someone a hundred years old … well, that's when we cause problems. It's okay for you. You like that stuff. You've got the brains for it.' Dyl folded up the canvas of the dismantled tent. He was good at it. It took him no time at all. 'But we like *doing* things. Working with our hands. This camp is great. It makes us feel like we don't always have to fail. That's why we behave.' He waved his hand around the clearing. 'I know these kids. And I can tell you they're all good, deep down.'

'What? Even John Oakman?' I asked.

'Well, not entirely sure about John,' admitted Dyl. He started putting the tent up again.

I thought about what he'd said. It proved two things, at

least. Firstly, Dyl was not dumb. I never thought he was, mind. That was just what everyone else thought. Secondly, it doesn't do to judge on appearances. Dyl was right. The retards. That's what other kids called them. I think, in private, it's what the teachers called them. But who was really dumb? The kids who acted up when forced to do things they couldn't accomplish, or those who condemned them for it without considering the reasons why? I was guilty of that.

Which all goes to prove, I guess, that I'm dumber than I like to think.

The rest of the day passed in a blur.

We had instructions on survival techniques, just in case we got lost out there. Phil and Jimmy told us that we wouldn't need it this time, because we were going to be travelling in a group and there'd be no chance of becoming separated. *That's what you think*, I said to myself. But the techniques might hold us in good stead for the future.

I paid particular attention. If Blacky was taking us into the bush, this information might save our lives. Blacky has many good qualities – well, I assume he has – but I suspected he wasn't going to come equipped with a GPS or an assortment of distress flares. Rolling in foul messes is all well and good, but it's rarely the difference between life and death.

Maybe I'm wrong, though. The last time I smelled Blacky I *wanted* to die.

We made lunch. Sandwiches and cordial. Then, in the afternoon, we played games. Instructional games, problem-

solving by communicating within the group. The sun made an appearance around two o'clock. It wasn't a warm sun, but it lifted our spirits.

It wasn't the only thing to make an appearance.

We had just started a trust-building exercise that involved falling backwards into the arms of a waiting team member. I'd been paired with John. This meant I had to stand a considerable distance away and catch something the size and weight of a mature ironbark tree. I was bracing myself, confident I'd be crushed like a bug, when an eerie sound drifted through the air.

'Cooeee.'

We all froze. What was that? The hairs on the back of my neck stood to attention and an icy chill ran down my spine. I gazed at the surrounding forest and an ominous silence gathered.

'Cooeee.'

Around a bend in the track, two people appeared, buried under a mass of camping equipment. They carried colossal rucksacks. Pots, pans and tents dangled from every available strap. I've seen department stores that weren't as well stocked. It wouldn't have surprised me to spot a five-burner gas barbecue with wok side-burner and an industrial fridge. They teetered towards us and stopped, the mountains on their backs swaying alarmingly. The gentle melody of tinkling pans faded and died.

'G'day!' said the mound on the right in a frighteningly cheerful voice.

It was, I think, a female mound. She wore glasses as thick as beer bottles which made her eyes look like pee-holes in the snow. They swam above a huge smile, exposing teeth like tombstones. If you'd stumbled across this apparition on a dark night it would have prompted an involuntary bowel movement. The other mound was probably male. It was difficult to tell.

'G'day,' said Phil, who was the first to recover his voice. 'Camping, huh?' he added, thus proving that nothing subtle gets past him.

'Absolutely,' said The Teeth. She leaned forward and lowered her voice. 'Actually, we are hunting.' If anything, her grin became wider. It was difficult to believe a human mouth could accommodate so many gnashers. Think of a very short-sighted beaver and you'll get the general idea.

'Really?' said Phil. 'And what are you hunting?'

'The thylacine.'

She'd lowered her voice even more, for reasons that weren't altogether clear. Did she think some government department might have bugged the forest? We were forced to lean closer.

'Ah,' said Phil, plucking at his earring. 'Caught many?'

'No,' she said seriously. 'We've been coming here every year for twenty years, determined to get photographic evidence. Plenty of close encounters, but no hard proof. But that's about to change. "This time, Gloria!" I said to myself. We can feel it, can't we, George?'

The other mound nodded, setting off another round of pot-clashing.

'Oh yes,' Gloria The Teeth continued. 'This is definitely the year. Well, mustn't dally. We heard your voices and thought we'd pop in to say hello. But time and the Tassie

77

tiger waits for no man. Onwards and upwards. Tally-ho and all that.'

'Good luck,' said Phil.

We watched as the mounds swayed noisily across the clearing and disappeared into the forest. I might have worried they'd get to the tiger before us, but it occurred to me that sneaking up on a wild animal stood a better chance of success if you didn't sound like a military brass band tuning up.

'Paira mad rocket mental numpties,' snarled Jimmy.

We made stew for dinner. Us kids peeled vegetables and Jimmy and Phil diced lumps of beef. We put the whole lot into a couple of huge pots and suspended them over the camp fire. Jimmy had kept some of the vegies separate and he put them into another pot with tofu chunks. Dinner wouldn't be ready for a couple of hours, but we were in no hurry. Once more, I felt bone-weary, but it was a good weariness.

As darkness drew in, we gathered round the fire. No one said much. We watched the flames and smelt the rich aroma of camp stew. I can't tell you how good it was.

Jimmy sat next to me. I glanced at him as he stared into the fire. Boy, was he hairy! My dad once put a roll of insulation into our roof space and it wasn't as thick as the mat on Jimmy's arms. An eagle could nest in it.

'Jimmy?' I said.

He turned his eyes towards me.

'Aye, lad.'

'Do you live out here?'

'I wish, laddie. I wish. Nay. Ye cannae live oot here. This is a state forest, so it is. Protected. If it wasnae, ev'ry Tom, Dick and bumhole wud be oot here, sticking up their wee hooses and cuttin' doon the trees to make room. And then there'd be TV towers and roods and Mc-freakin'-Donalds. And ye know whit, laddie?'

I shook my head. He leaned in closer.

'Then all of this wud be gone,' he whispered. 'Everything. An' that … that wud be a crime, so it wud.'

'You love this place, don't you?'

'Aye. I do that.'

'So it *is* protected, at least.'

Jimmy sighed.

'In theory, laddie. In theory.'

'What do you mean?'

'Huv a butchers aroond ye, lad. What do ya see?'

'Butchers?'

'A look. What d'ye see all aroond us?'

'Trees.'

'Aye, lad. Trees. Living things. Magnificent. Ancient. But if, God forbid, we had a business peerson here, do ye know what *they'd* see? They'd see money, lad. Money. Profit. More bucks i'the bank, so they could buy another car or build another hoose. 'Cause there's money in timber, son. There's awfay money in timber.'

He scratched his nose.

'Course, we have politicians to run things.' He spat into the fire. It hissed. 'Trouble is, a politician loves a businessman, so he does. Thick as thieves. So when a businessman wants tae cut doon trees there's plenty o' pollies who willnae

get i'the way. We need tae be vigilant, son. *You* need tae be vigilant.'

'Me?'

'Aye, you. Us auld uns huv hud oor time and a right pig's ear we've made of it. It's you weans that huv to look oot fi the world noo. If it's not already too late.'

I watched the fire and thought. Tasmania was freezing cold and where we were you couldn't get reception on your mobile phone. But it was so beautiful.

And like many beautiful things, so fragile.

'GET UP! NOW!'

I shook my head. Was I never going to be allowed to sleep? I struggled up in bed and glanced at the luminous dials of my watch. Three-thirty in the morning. What was going on?

'You need to get dressed, tosh. Wake Dylan. It's time.'

I rubbed at my eyes.

'Blacky,' I said. 'Are you some kind of mad rocket numpty?' I was beginning to pick up Jimmy's way of talking. They say it's easier to learn a foreign language when you're young. 'It's the middle of the night. Surely it can wait until morning?'

'No, mush. It's an emergency.'

'What is?'

There was silence for a couple of seconds.

'She's sick,' said Blacky. 'Really sick.'

'Who is?'

'The last Tasmanian tiger. There's no time to waste, boyo. Not if we want to have a chance of saving her.'

Dyl woke as soon as I put a hand on his shoulder. His eyes widened.

'Marc,' he whispered. 'You're scaring me.'

'Sorry, mate,' I whispered back. 'But Blacky is here. We have to go. Now.'

'No. Not that,' he said, swinging his legs out of bed and reaching for his clothes. 'It's you. *You're* scaring me.'

I realised why. I was wearing my thermal underwear. I'd snuck it on when I'd got under the covers last night. Now I was standing in the dorm looking like a pale grey sausage. *Never mind*, I thought. *I'm going to be grateful I've got them.*

We got dressed in less than thirty seconds. I grabbed the backpack next to my bed. Jimmy and Phil had insisted we stow our gear ready for the morning hike. According to Jimmy, they didn't want us faffin' aboot for hours like a wee buncha galoots and boggin' muppets. Wise words, I thought. Or was it *meaningless* words? Anyway, the backpack

contained the tent, wet-weather gear and a survival pack, including emergency rations.

Dyl and I crept out of the dorm. The floorboards creaked a couple of times and we stopped and listened. It was unlikely any of the other kids would wake up. If yesterday was anything to go by, they were so tired they'd sleep through a marching band recital with an accompanying fireworks display.

It was a bitter night. There was a half-moon nestled in the branches of trees. The clearing around the cabins was bathed in pale, cold light.

Blacky was by the barbecue. Dyl and I padded over to him, hoisting our backpacks onto our shoulders.

'Let's go,' he said.

'Wait a moment, Blacky,' I said. 'I have to leave a message.'

He made snuffling, impatient noises in my head. I can't even begin to tell you how weird that was.

'Why, mush? What's the point?'

'They'll worry, Blacky. I need to tell them we're safe, that we haven't been abducted. Say we'll join up with them here in a few days.'

'Oh, okay, tosh. That'll really work. *Me and Dyl, twelve years old and city boys, have wandered off into hostile bush in a remote wilderness area for reasons best known to ourselves. Don't wait up.* That'll put their minds at rest! They *are* going to search for you, mush. You know that, don't you? Probably with police, mountain rescue and helicopters. And you are also going to have to avoid being discovered. Until the mission is completed.'

I knew all that. But when he put it that way, I suddenly

realised how much trouble I was going to be in. Mum and Dad would be informed. They'd go mental. And it wasn't just them. There were so many people who'd be worried sick about our safety. Rose would be distraught at my disappearance. Who was she going to torture if I wasn't around?

And I'd never be able to explain. Not without the risk of being checked into the nearest lunatic asylum. Perhaps I should say nothing. Let them think we *had* been kidnapped. Claim amnesia and then pretend to forget I'd claimed it. That might be a way to avoid being deep in the brown, smelly stuff for the rest of my days.

I couldn't, though. I had to leave some message.

Now, I don't know about you, but if you've ever got up at three-thirty in the morning in the middle of nowhere to chase after an extinct animal, you might have had the foresight to pack a writing pad and pencil. Not me. I had nothing to write with.

So I took a stick and scratched a message in the dirt next to the barbecue.

*Please don't worry. We are safe. Will be back.*

Blacky was right. It wouldn't work. But I felt better having done it. I hoped it wasn't going to rain and wash the message away. Actually, I was hoping it wasn't going to rain anyway. I was freezing as it was.

Blacky led the way out of the clearing. I glanced back. I could just make out the cabins, bathed in soft moonlight. They were solid, safe. Then the bush swallowed us and they were gone.

Within five minutes we were deep into the forest and the moon was hidden by overarching trees. The darkness was thick. It pressed on my eyes.

There was a torch among the survival gear, but Blacky wouldn't let me turn it on.

'If anyone back at the camp woke up, they'd be able to see the beam. We need to move in darkness for at least half an hour. You can use it then.'

It was the worst half-hour of my life and I've had a few bad ones in my time. Mainly involving Rose.

I couldn't see a metre in front of me, even after my eyes had adjusted to the night. We moved slowly in single file. Blacky in the lead, then me and Dyl bringing up the rear. There was no path as far as I could tell. We picked our way through trees, occasionally tripping over fallen branches. But that wasn't the scariest bit. Whenever we stopped, the bush was alive with rustles, scratches, sounds of unseen things moving all around. Once, something startled only a metre away to my right. A dark shape, a wedge of shadow among shadows, plunged into the bush with a crash that brought my stomach, my heart and most of my internal organs up into my throat.

Another reason to be grateful for the thermal underwear. They were so tight that if I *did* poop myself in terror, there was no chance anything nasty would slide down my trouser leg and deposit itself in my shoe.

Partly to mask the sounds of animals, I told Dyl what Blacky had said about the last Tasmanian tiger. I kept my voice down. I don't know why, but there, in the heart of the bush, it felt like being in church.

'Sick?' whispered Dyl. 'With what?'

Blacky chipped in.

'According to Tess—'

'Tess?' I said.

'Tess, the Tassie tiger. She was walking through the bush when she caught a scent. Human scent. She froze in fear. The presence of humans does that to animals. When she turned her head, she saw the guy about twenty metres away. She ran but he followed. And then there was another human to her left trying to cut her off. Eventually, they backed her onto a small cliff. Her only chance of escape was to jump.'

'What happened?' I asked.

'She fell badly, broke a hind leg. But at least the men couldn't get to her. Not without going a long way round. Tess took the opportunity to crawl away. Four or five kilometres in all. She found a place to hide. But those hunters will not give up. It's been over a week. They'll find her, if we don't get to her first.'

I passed all this on to Dyl.

'That's so sad,' he said. 'If someone sees a Tassie tiger – the last tiger in the world – why would they hunt her down? Isn't it enough just to have *seen* her?'

'Apparently not,' said Blacky. 'I imagine there's plenty of money to be made by catching the last tiger in the world. And fame, of course. You humans can't resist fame and fortune. I just wonder what you'll do when you've finished destroying the entire earth. You might be famous and rich. But that won't make crops grow. Or bring back a single living thing you've destroyed.'

'Not all humans are like that, Blacky,' I said.

'No,' he agreed. 'Not all. But – unfortunately for the future of the world – enough.'

I couldn't argue with that.

'So you want us to fix her broken leg? That's the mission?' I thought about it. I knew you had to do something with splints, keep the leg encased in a rigid structure until the bones healed properly. I just wasn't sure I had the skill.

'I can do that,' said Dyl. I realised I had been talking out loud. 'That's part of the curriculum for the special boys unit. First aid. I've got a certificate.'

'That *was* the mission,' said Blacky. 'But now it's more complicated. We have more to worry about than a broken leg.'

'What?'

'You'll see,' Blacky said. 'But time is running out. We must hurry.'

I pulled out the torch from my backpack.

'Then a little light won't hurt,' I said.

I snapped the switch on the torch and a broad beam of light illuminated a huge tree.

And then it died.

The beam, not the tree. Though if it had, I wouldn't have been able to see it.

I joggled the switch. I shook the torch. I bounced it a couple of times against the palm of my hand. Stop me if I'm getting too technical here. But whatever I did, the torch remained lifeless. It was a worry. If everything else in the pack was similarly made, my emergency supplies would probably be a few woodchips and matches made of asbestos. At least the tent worked. I knew that from considerable experience.

Dyl pulled his torch out. That didn't work either.

'Fabulous,' I said. 'About as much use as a chocolate teapot. Blacky, we might be in a rush, but until dawn arrives we are going to have to creep through this forest.'

'Terrific, tosh,' snorted Blacky. 'What is it with humans and their senses? You couldn't find your own bum in a darkroom if it had a bell on it. Deaf as rocks, a sense of smell as acute as the average refrigerator's and blind as bats. Actually, that is a great insult to bats, who can navigate in total darkness on account of their use of sonar—'

'Yeah, all right, Blacky,' I replied. 'At least we can see in colour, which dogs can't.'

'Oh yes. Very useful under these circumstances. Exactly what colour *is* the black all around you, then?'

I sighed.

'I'm just saying ...'

'Hang on!'

There was silence, broken by a faint rustle in the bush off to my right. I could sense Blacky's concentration. There was something out there. Something that he found very interesting.

'What is it, Blacky?' I whispered in my head. I have no idea why I was whispering in my head. It seemed a natural thing to do. 'Is it dangerous?'

My head was full of images of powerful, sleek bodies moving purposefully through the night. Sharp, yellowed teeth. Razor-like claws. Padding towards us.

The silence stretched.

'Stay here,' hissed Blacky eventually. 'I need to investigate. Don't move a step.'

And he was gone.

'Blacky!' I yelled. 'What is it? Where are you?'

But there was no reply. The skittering in the undergrowth was louder now. And getting closer. I stretched out my hand and touched Dyl on the arm. It was comforting to make contact with someone who didn't understand the concept of fear. Not that that would prevent him from being ripped to pieces, I reminded myself. He'd just be cool about it. I, on the other hand, would fill my thermal underwear.

'What's happening, Marc?' said Dyl.

I explained that Blacky had gone to investigate something urgent.

'It's getting lighter, mate.'

He was right. The darkness was patched with grey. I could still see nothing. But I could see slightly more nothing than before. It was a relief. I was hungry, tired, cold and wet with morning dew. I could do without the additional blindness.

So when Dylan took a step backwards, I didn't exactly *see* him, unless you count the shift and blur of a wedge of darkness across my eyes. It was more sensing it. What I *didn't* have to sense was his cry of alarm and his hand slipping across the fabric of my jacket. I tried to grab him but it was too late. Without thinking, I took a step towards where he had been.

Something slipped and gave under my shoes. I wind-milled backwards, tried to keep my balance. But the ground dissolved beneath me. I felt a small rush of soil and stones under my footing and then nothing.

I fell.

In an emergency, I suppose the body does things without being conscious of it.

I twisted and flung my hands forwards, scrabbled at the ground. For a moment, my fingers dug in and I hung precariously over the unseen drop. Then the soil shifted and sieved through my grasp. Centimetre by centimetre, I slipped further over the edge.

For all I knew, the drop beneath me was less than a metre. Maybe I'd fall, yelling and shrieking, for a tenth of a second. Land on Dyl. But it *felt* as though I was on the edge of the world. Somehow I knew that if I fell, my plunge would last forever.

I've heard that, on the point of death, people become calm, accepting of their fate.

It's not true.

Beads of sweat formed on my forehead, despite the bitter cold. They ran into my eyes and stung. My arms were on fire and my fingers, hard as steel, were digging, digging, slipping. My life did *not* flash before my eyes. Just as well. Most of it had involved being tortured by Rose and I certainly didn't want the last thing I'd ever see to be her ugly mug.

I could feel the strength draining from me. My fingers uncurling. Slowly. I shifted another centimetre. I had only seconds left.

A hand grasped my wrist just as my fingers clutched at thin air. I didn't stop to wonder. I kicked my feet in front of me, found a solid surface, scrabbled to gain a foothold. Whoever had hold of me strained to take my weight, pull me up.

It was still progress that could be measured in centimetres, but this time I was heading in the right direction.

Finally, I managed to hook my elbows over the edge of the drop and squirm my way to safety. When I stood my legs felt as if they were made of rubber. I nearly collapsed. And not just because of fear. It was getting lighter by the second and I could make out the identity of my rescuer.

John Oakman towered over me.

I had questions, but they could wait.

I flung myself on my belly and yelled out over the drop. Despite the brightening dawn, I couldn't see anything.

'Dyl!' I screamed.

There was silence for a heartbeat or two. All I could hear was the rush of blood in my ears and the faint echo of my voice mocking me. Then the sound came. Faint.

'Yo, Marc! What's going down, dude?'

*You, apparently*, I thought. I almost said it as well, the relief was so great.

'Where are you, Dyl? I can't see anything.'

'Me neither, mate. As far as I can tell, I'm floating.'

Floating? He must have been hysterical.

'Don't worry, Dyl,' I shouted. 'Help is on its way.'

'I'm not worried, Marc,' came the reply. 'It's kinda cool floating here. Take your time.'

I hadn't quite worked out what help I was talking about, let alone how it was on its way, but I thought it important to keep his spirits up. Not that Dylan's spirits ever get down. Not even when he does a plunge over a cliff face. The only good thing, apart from the fact he was obviously still alive, was that the light was growing stronger. It would only be a matter of minutes before I could see where he was and assess the situation better.

In the meantime I found a rock and tossed it over the edge. I was careful to throw it well away from Dyl's voice. He wouldn't be too happy to be brained with a large rock. Though, with Dyl, you could never be sure about stuff like that. I listened for the sound of the rock hitting the bottom. Nothing. This was not a good sign.

I waited. John Oakman lay by my side and we both peered into darkness. Until Dyl was safe I didn't want to talk, but the silence was unsettling. My nerves were shot. So I figured this was a good time to get an answer or two. A conversation would help the minutes tick away.

'John, what the hell are you doing here?'

'Saw you leave, Mucus. Followed.'

As always, John dished out words as if they were in short supply and likely to run out at any moment. He spat each one out. Cold and hard, like marbles.

'Why?'

'You. Can't escape me.'

It was testimony to John's hatred that he was prepared to get up in the middle of a freezing cold night and track me through a hostile forest in the pitch dark. It couldn't have been easy following us. Then I spotted the flaw.

'So why did you rescue me then, John?'

He mulled this one over. It was as though I'd asked him to explain Einstein's Theory of Relativity. Most questions

93

are tricky for John. Asking him his name is liable to short-circuit a few neural synapses and cause smoke to issue from his ears.

'You. Don't escape that easy,' he said, just when I was beginning to give up hope of an answer.

*Easy?* I shuddered to think what he had in mind, if hurling yourself off a cliff was too simple.

Luckily, I didn't have time to consider the implications. The gloom had cleared and I could see what we had to deal with. To be honest, when I could see, I wished I couldn't.

Firstly, the drop wasn't a metre. More like two hundred. Far beneath, a river wound its slow course through the bottom of a gorge. If John hadn't grabbed me…

The second reason was Dyl. He'd fallen about ten metres. Straight onto a gnarled tree that had managed to attach roots to the sides of the gorge. The top strap on his backpack had miraculously become entangled in the branches. No wonder he felt like he was floating. He swung gently over the drop like some kind of peculiar fruit. He had his arms stretched out as if flying. In one hand was an open can of cola.

My relief that he was alive turned to despair. How were we going to get him out of that tree without sending him to certain death? Then I heard a ripping sound. Dyl must have been travelling fast when he hit the tree, because the stitching on the strap was coming apart. Even as I watched, a piece of canvas unpeeled from its seam and he sagged a few more centimetres.

'Far out,' yelled Dyl. 'This is mad fun.'

Two kids. No equipment. No time to get help. The only thing I agreed with was the 'mad' part.

I turned my face towards John. He could probably read the horror in it, but I didn't care.

John jumped to his feet and dug his hand down into his pocket. He unravelled a spool of white material from its depths and started paying it out. I watched. It seemed to be cord of some kind. Thin cord.

'John,' I said. 'If you're thinking of rescuing Dyl with that, you can forget it.' It would be like winding a length of string around an elephant and trying to use it as a yoyo.

'Parachute cord,' he said. 'Strong.'

I wondered why John would be carrying parachute cord around with him. Then I remembered his career ambition and figured he kept it on him to experiment with. Whatever, I was grateful. If he ever needed a referee in his application for Official Hangman of Australia, I'd be happy to oblige.

John tied one end round a sturdy tree trunk and let the other end out over the edge of the cliff until it dangled in front of Dyl's face. Even as Dyl reached to grab it, the seam on his backpack split a little further. John gave clipped instructions on how to tie the cord around his waist, using a secure knot. Dyl had no sooner done so than the seam finally gave way and the strap ripped loose.

I watched, frozen in horror, as Dyl slammed into the cliff face.

The torn backpack rocked in the branches for a couple of seconds before fluttering down into the gorge. I watched it, a strange denim butterfly, until it shrank to a dot and disappeared.

John and I snapped out of our trance at the same time, rushed back to the tree and started pulling on the cord. I found it hard to believe that something as slender and fragile-looking as cotton could take his weight. It was difficult to get a grip, and it bit into our palms. But Dyl was obviously finding handholds and footholds on the cliff face, because we managed to pull up the cord, metre after slow metre. I have never felt so relieved as when Dyl's hands finally popped over the edge of the cliff, followed quickly by his face. He was grinning.

He flopped onto safety. John and I dragged him a few metres away from the drop. We lay, panting and exhausted, for a few moments.

'Let's do it again,' said Dyl.

I was about to throttle him with my bare hands. If he wanted another near-death experience I was just in the mood to oblige. But I didn't get the chance. A voice boomed in my head.

'Oi, mush! If you've quite finished having a rest, we need to get on. I dunno! Humans. Always thinking of your comfort. And who's the beanpole twonk?'

I struggled to my feet. Blacky stood in front of me.

And then the smell hit.

I staggered back a couple of paces, nearly went for another double twist with pike off the edge of the cliff, and stopped myself just in time.

Though the stench was so bad, maybe I should have gone for it.

'Blacky!' I yelled. 'That is the most disgusting thing I've ever smelled. And I've spent considerable time in your company, remember.'

'Thanks, tosh. It's a good one, isn't it? Rotting wallaby carcass. Soon as I smelled it, I knew I had to have it. Nearly as good as that fruit bat in Queensland. The combination of maggots and decomposition …'

I held up my hand.

'Way too much information, Blacky,' I said. 'And let me get this right. You took off, not because there was an emergency, but because you wanted to roll in something dead?'

'It *was* an emergency, mush. It was like winning the lotto. No dog could pass up that chance. Anyway, we weren't going anywhere, because you couldn't see. Remember?'

'Blacky, *bucko*, we fell off this cliff! While you were getting yourself a makeover, me and Dyl nearly died!'

Blacky trotted over to the edge and gazed down.

'I told you not to move a step, tosh. What part of "don't move" did you have trouble understanding? Sorry, mush.

Not my fault you have the intellect of an earthworm and can't follow simple instructions.'

I was really tempted to give him a toe-end over the cliff. My foot twitched.

Blacky cocked his head.

'And you haven't answered my question. Who's the long and ugly streak of pee?'

I glanced at John. His head was moving backwards and forwards, from me to Blacky. It was easy to see why he was confused. A dog in the wilderness? Doesn't compute. I watched out for telltale wisps of smouldering brain matter coming out of his lug-holes, but couldn't spot any.

'Why?' said John.

'Sorry, mate,' I replied. 'I might need more information before I can answer that one.'

'You. Staring at dog. Dog staring at you. Why?'

It must have appeared bizarre. Dyl, of course, was used to it, but to John it must have seemed as if Blacky and I had hypnotised each other. Or fallen in love. I almost threw up at the thought, though that might have had something to do with the smell that rolled off Blacky in foul waves. Luckily, I kept my stomach safely gathered in. I'd had enough of diced carrots. I imagine John felt the same.

'It's a long story, mate,' I said. 'Anyway, it's been fun, but it's time you went back to camp. Dyl and I are going for a little walk. Back soon. Say hi to everyone. Don't save us any breakfast.'

'No.'

'Sorry? You *will* save us breakfast?'

'No.'

'You wouldn't care to elaborate on that, John?'

'No.'

'You can't come with us.'

'Can. Will.'

I sighed and turned to Dylan.

'You explain, Dyl.'

Dyl took me by the arm and led me away a few metres. I glanced back. John and Blacky were eyeing each other. Neither seemed impressed. If it had been Kyle instead of John, it might have worked out. They could have taken it in turns to roll in each other.

'Not goin' to work, mate,' said Dyl. 'If John's got it into his head to follow us, he will. Anyway, he saved my life. We can't send him away, even if he'd listen. Which he won't.'

'He saved my life, too,' I said. 'But he can't come on this mission, Dyl. He mustn't know about Blacky or the Tassie tiger.'

Dyl shrugged.

'Okay. But we've not got much choice. Like it or not, he's a part of this mission now.'

I sighed. He was right. But I was not happy. Neither was Blacky. He'd got the whole story from reading my mind. He didn't sigh. He snarled.

Dyl and I trailed Blacky through the forest. John trailed us.

Look. I'm a huge fan of Nature. If it released a cd I would be first in line to buy it. I'd follow it on Twitter. I'd go and see it live. I *was* seeing it live. But, after four or five hours of trudging through the same type of landscape, I was becoming tired, physically and emotionally.

'How much further, Blacky?' I asked.

'About a day,' he replied.

'WHAAAT? You can't be serious.' I was flabbergasted. Never, in my short life, had something gasted my flabber so completely.

'Do I sound like a stand-up comedian, boyo?'

'But what are we going to eat?'

'I thought that pack on your shoulders had provisions.'

It did, though I hadn't had time to check them out before. Emergency rations. Maybe it was one of those things where you poured water on a pill and it transformed into a roast chicken with gravy, mashed potatoes and stuffing. Knowing my luck, it'd probably have Brussels sprouts as well. Dyl's backpack, of course, was at the bottom of a gorge and John, I noticed, hadn't brought his along at all.

Survival food for one would have to stretch three ways.

There'd be one tent for three of us. Not Blacky. I would barricade the flap and set up an electronic burglar alarm before I let that smelly mutt in. Then again, we'd probably wake up in the morning – freezing cold and starving – and find he'd spent the night in a five-star hotel with cable TV, gourmet food and a jacuzzi.

We stopped for lunch around noon.

I say lunch, but my hopes about the freeze-dried roast or a pill that would change into a Black Forest gateau turned out to be wildly optimistic. There were granola bars. High-energy, apparently. Low-taste, certainly. It was like chewing cat litter. Not that I've ever eaten cat litter.

Well, yeah, okay. Once. But I was two years old. The cat scratched me as well.

101

After lunch, just for a welcome change, we walked through forest. My feet were getting blisters. My blisters were getting blisters. The straps of my backpack were digging into my shoulders. All of my muscles ached.

At least there was plenty of water. We often stumbled across small streams; the water was pure, cold and fresh. I had a water bottle attached to my pack and we drank as much as we could and then filled the bottle. You never knew if that was the last stream you'd ever see.

The sun was low when we found a small clearing and set up camp. Dyl and John gathered dry wood while I found some large stones. The talk that Jimmy and Phil had given turned out useful. I arranged the stones in a circle and we broke up some of the smaller twigs into kindling and placed them in the centre. The matches in the survival pack worked, which was a relief.

When the fire caught properly, we fed it bigger branches. Soon there was a roaring blaze. The four of us sat around it. Gradually, warmth returned. Nobody said much, but you couldn't call our camp exactly quiet. For one thing, there was the sound of night-time critters stirring in the bush. For another there was the loud crackle of burning branches. But drowning all that was the sound of three stomachs rumbling. Blacky was okay. Maybe he'd brought along his stash of dried beef. But the rest of us were starving. Just as well the last Tasmanian tiger didn't happen to stroll into our clearing. We'd have had it skinned and roasting in two shakes of a lamb's willie, which wouldn't exactly have helped our mission.

After an hour of gazing moodily into the fire, we put up

the tent. We were exhausted. Dyl, John and I stared at the space inside. It was the size of a welcome mat, but not as inviting.

'If anyone farts,' I said, 'we are in real trouble.'

Getting inside the tent was a problem. Dyl went first and scrunched himself up against the side. I went next and took up the other wall of the tent. This left a space of about six centimetres between us for John. He was thin, true, but not that thin. By the time he'd winkled himself in we were like sardines in a can.

We smelt like them, too.

No shower and a full day of walking through the forest. Not to mention sweaty brushes with death on a cliff's edge.

Maybe a fart *would* improve things.

John's legs stretched outside the tent flaps. We'd pitched it close to the fire, thinking we'd need the warmth. But three bodies generated enough heat to do without it. As I tried to sleep, I wondered if John's legs would fall across the dying embers and barbecue themselves overnight.

At least it would take care of breakfast.

It was a restless night. I'd wake up and wonder where I was. Then it would all come flooding back and I'd try to get my nose out of John's armpit. If anyone moved, everyone woke. This did nothing for our mood.

Once, I woke and thought I saw something moving just outside the tent. I blinked groggily.

'Blacky?' I said in my head. 'Is that you?'

No reply.

And then I saw it. Correction. I *think* I saw it. Between the flaps of the tent. A head. Thin, long jaws stretched in a grim smile. Rows of sharp teeth. I jolted upright and the violence of my action snapped Dyl and John to attention. John nearly put a hole in the tent's roof with his head.

'What the …' said Dyl.

There was nothing there. I stared at the opening in the tent. Blank. No sudden shifting of an animal alarmed at our movement. I must have imagined it. A nightmare.

'Sorry, guys,' I said. 'I thought I saw something.'

We settled down and I closed my eyes. When I opened them a moment later, John's face was a centimetre from mine. His eyes bored into me. I nearly jolted upright again.

'You will, Mucus,' he croaked.

'What?' I whispered.

'See something. My fist. In your eye.'

On that cheerful note, I drifted off. The day had been a disaster. We were starving, wet and alternately freezing cold and suffocatingly warm. Surely things would improve tomorrow?

If I'd known what the next day held, I probably wouldn't have slept at all.

I was woken by the sound of helicopter blades.

At first I didn't pay much attention, tried to brush the noise away as if it was an irritating fly. Then my eyes snapped open. At the same time, I heard Blacky's voice in my head.

'Hurry, tosh. They're coming for you.'

Jimmy and Phil! It had been a day since we left. They would have searched for an hour or so by themselves. The note I'd left wouldn't have stopped them. Now the approaching helicopter told me they'd enlisted help.

We got the tent down in thirty seconds, brushed away the remains of the camp fire and found shelter among the trees. The thrumming of the blades swelled to a roar, then faded. I let out my breath. I hadn't realised I'd been holding it.

I made to go back out to the clearing, but John Oakman took me by the arm.

'Why, Mucus?' he said.

It was a fair question. I knew that. And I knew he deserved an answer. I just couldn't give him one.

'I can't tell you, John,' I said. 'Sorry. But me and Dyl can't go back. Not yet. We have something important to do. But *you* can, mate. Stay here in the clearing, light another fire. Put on plenty of green leaves. The smoke'll bring the helicopter back. You could be eating breakfast in an hour.' The thought of breakfast made my stomach rumble again.

John fixed me with his eyes. They were light blue. I hadn't noticed the colour of his eyes before.

'No,' he said. 'Go with you.'

'But, John …'

'Go with you.' His tone wasn't firm. It was set in concrete. There was no point arguing.

I stashed the tent away in my backpack. Ten minutes after waking, we were ready for another fascinating trek in the wilderness. Blacky once more led the way. The three of us trailed behind him. We didn't talk. We were still tired. No. Weary. Starving. The day stretched before us and held no promise.


'People!' whispered Dyl. 'I hear voices.'

I almost bumped into him. I had been walking asleep and everything in the outside world had merged into a dream. Now I stopped. John, in turn, almost bumped into me. I had no idea where Blacky was. It took a moment or two for me to focus. Dyl was right. Voices. There were people ahead.

Dylan padded softly forward, put his head around a tree. John and I followed.

We had stumbled upon a clearing and in its centre were two mounds of camping equipment on legs. Two familiar mounds.

Our tiger hunters had obviously stopped to have lunch. Remnants of food were scattered across a picnic blanket. George and Gloria stood about ten metres away from the blanket. They were examining a map.

'What should we do, Blacky?' I whispered. 'Skirt around them? We could head into the forest, then circle back. They wouldn't hear us.'

I have no idea what Blacky's response would have been because at that moment the tiger hunters turned their backs to us. Tombstone Teeth tapped the map and pointed into the bush. Dyl, meanwhile, slipped out from behind the tree and headed straight towards them. I tried to catch his arm but it was too late. I couldn't even call out.

What an idiot! He was going to blow everything.

Dyl moved almost soundlessly across the intervening ground, and stopped at the picnic blanket. Then I realised what he was doing. Food!

What a genius! He was going to save our lives.

Now, I don't want to give the impression I think stealing is okay. It isn't. But we were starving and they obviously had plenty of provisions. My conscience was rumbling. But my stomach was rumbling louder.

Dylan crouched at the blanket for a few seconds then spun away and raced back. I held my breath. My face must have been so purple you could have mistaken me for an eggplant. Only when he slipped behind our tree did I let my breath out. Dyl grinned triumphantly and held out a large bottle of cola.

What an *idiot*!

John and I stared at him.

'I'm going to kill you, Dyl,' I whispered.

I even went to put my hands around his neck, but John stopped me. 'No, Mucus,' he said. 'Can't kill Dyl.'

This struck me as generous from someone whose life's ambition was to suffocate people. I looked upon John with renewed respect.

'*I* kill him,' he continued, reaching for Dyl's neck with *his* hands. Dylan probably wouldn't have resisted. That would have meant dropping the cola and I suspect you would have needed a chisel to pry it from his grasp.

Luckily, death was averted. When Dyl realised that John and I considered *food* to be essential to survival – I suspect he thought we were being eccentric – he legged it back and returned with a couple of foil-wrapped packages. Our tiger hunters remained blissfully unaware. I reckon we could have removed their underdaks and they wouldn't have noticed. Given they were hoping to sneak up on the most elusive creature in Australia, their inability to spot Dyl at five paces didn't inspire confidence.

We ripped the packages open.

Sandwiches.

Cheese and tomato sandwiches.

Look, I would have eaten them if they'd been Brussels sprouts sandwiches.

We tore into the food like wild animals.

It's amazing how much better I felt with something in my stomach. I rolled up the sandwich foil and put it into my pocket. Then I stowed the empty cola bottle into my backpack. I don't litter. Not since I found out how much damage it does to the environment.

Time to get moving again. I took a couple of paces and then heard another set of voices.

Behind us, this time.

Close.

What was going on? I was beginning to wonder how a wilderness area could become so crowded. At the rate it was going we could organise our own full-strength rugby match. Including spectators.

'Hide!' hissed Blacky's voice in my head.

Trouble was, where? The voices behind were so close that taking off sideways into the bush would have been a dead giveaway. And we couldn't move quietly away from the voices without running straight into the tiger hunters. I glanced up. The tree we were under had no branches close to the ground.

That left only one direction.

Down.

I don't think I would have been able to burrow into the undergrowth if I hadn't just had an injection of cheese-and-tomato-sandwich energy. In ten seconds, the three of us were nestled under a carpet of twigs, yellowed leaves and rotting vegetation. Three seconds later the owners of the voices stopped right beside us.

Jimmy and Mr Crannitch.

You are probably amazed at my powers of deduction, since we were completely covered. And quite right, too. You see, I was staring at a boot only a few centimetres from my eye. I had to squint through a gap in the leaves. But, even with limited vision, I could tell by the small scratches and scuffs that this boot belonged to a person who spent

109

time outdoors. The tufts of springy hair poking out at the ankle indicated the owner was genetically comparable to an orang-utan. The rest was elementary for someone of my intellect. Sherlock Holmes could have taken my correspondence course.

Then again, Jimmy was yelling. That may have provided a small clue.

'Ah dinnae ken where those boggin' weans huv got tae. Gies a break, an' at. Knaw what ah mean, eh?'

Mr Crannitch was obviously still ill, because his words were slurred.

'Oh, my God. Three! I've losht three kids. Wassa school goin' to shay? Wassa parents goin' to shay?'

'Och, quit yer greetin, stop bumpin' yer gums an' put a sock in yer bletherin, ya galoot. We cannae give up oan 'em yetawhile.'

It would have been fascinating to follow this conversation further, if only to see whether I could understand *anything* Jimmy said. But at that moment the Scotsman lifted his boot and brought it down on my outstretched fingers. I choked back a scream. Jimmy might be small but he packed weight. It felt like my hand was on fire. Then Mr Crannitch shifted his foot and brought it down on my other hand. Pinned to the ground by two gibberish-speaking adults, I discovered I'd lost my powers of concentration.

There was more talking, accompanied by grinding of heels into my bruised and battered pinkies. Through the haze of pain, I managed to gather some information. Apparently, search parties were combing the gorge for our remains. They'd found Dyl's ripped, battered backpack and jumped to conclusions. But Jimmy, it seemed, wasn't convinced. He'd followed a trail *away* from the cliff's edge and taken Mr Crannitch with him. Phil, I imagined, was looking after the rest of the group.

At this stage, my fingers felt as if they'd been clamped in a vice and then had acid poured over them. To make matters worse, an ant had crawled up my left nostril in search of quality accommodation and a sneeze was building. I fought to control it. The pressure in my head was such that I worried the top of my skull would explode, spewing brains into the air like a volcanic eruption. And being splattered with grey matter might alert Jimmy and Mr C to our hiding place.

Luckily they noticed the tiger hunters at this point and moved away. Thirty seconds later, we heard the low murmur of conversation, punctuated occasionally by bursts of high-decibel gibberish from Jimmy. I flexed my fingers and wondered whether I would be able to play the piano. I hoped so. I'd never been able to play it before.

We lay for ten minutes while the ant continued to explore my nostril. It was probably considering where to set up its plasma TV with surround-sound and what colour to repaint the walls.

The buzz of conversation was brief. Then we heard the tinkle of pots and pans fading into the distance. Jimmy's voice dwindled and died.

Silence.

'Hurry up, tosh,' came Blacky's voice. 'Time is running out.'

We jumped up from our hiding place and brushed leaves from our clothes. I carefully evicted the ant from my nose and placed it on the ground. It wasn't keen to leave. In fact, I suspect it was calling its mates to tell them it had found the perfect apartment. Vacant, apart from the odd booger, and with exceptionally reasonable rent. What's more, there was another one next door.

Blacky appeared at our feet. He cocked his head and fixed me with those pink-rimmed eyes.

'We have to run, mush. She's fading fast. It might be too late already. No more creeping around.'

And then he was gone, a dirty-white blur across the track.

'Run, guys,' I said. 'Follow the hound.'

We pounded through bush. Blacky moved so fast it was difficult to track him. I shouted in my head but he didn't let up the pace. Within five minutes, the trees thinned and we entered a large clearing.

This land was dotted with bushes and the undergrowth was thick with coarse grass that came to my knees. Blacky had virtually disappeared beneath its surface. It was only by following the movement of the grass that I was able to track his route. By now, my breath was ragged and my heart thumping. And not just from exercise. Blacky's words echoed in my head. *Fading fast. Too late already.* Tears stung my eyes and I had no idea where they'd come from. I brushed them aside with one arm and redoubled my efforts.

We passed over a slight ridge and came to a stop.

Blacky lay panting ten metres in front of us. He was next to a low, dense bush. The grass around the area was flattened, which was why we could see him. I took one step forward. The grass was badged in dark brown splodges.

Blood. Dried blood.

I took another pace.

I wanted so badly to see.

I wanted so badly *not* to see.

Blacky said nothing.

I moved slowly behind the bush. There was no animal, but there was a smell. A sickly, powerful smell of rottenness, of corruption. I knelt down and put one hand over my nose, the other hand towards the thick shrub. Close up, I could see that something had crawled in there.

I trembled as I parted the branches.

She lay on her side. Fawn-coloured with ten, maybe fifteen, chocolate-brown stripes from a stiff tail to halfway up her spine.

Her eyes met mine and she lifted her head slightly, but the effort was too much and she slumped back. I looked down at her hind leg.

It was a mess. A jagged splinter of bone jutted through fur. It must have been incredibly painful, but I knew that was the least of her worries. I knew because the source of the smell was now obvious. Her entire leg was puffy, swollen with infection. I'd heard of this. The word burst into my mind like a bomb.

*Gangrene.*

The tiger's chest rose and fell in short, rapid movements.

Suddenly, the tears that had started during my run welled up afresh. I sat back on my heels and sobbed. I rocked backwards and forwards and sobbed. Dyl and John knelt beside me. I felt their arms around my shoulders. Never before had I felt such desolation.

When Blacky's words came, they were uncharacteristically gentle.

'You didn't do this to her, tosh.'

'No,' I cried in my mind. 'I didn't. But other human beings made her like this. By tracking her down, making her desperate. And that makes me responsible, in part. And ashamed. I am so ashamed, Blacky.'

'I didn't bring you here to feel shame, Marc. This is a mission, mush, not another example of how badly humans treat the world. There is still good to be done.'

I ran my hands through my hair.

'But how, Blacky? Me and Dyl can't deal with this. The broken leg, maybe. But this infection…her leg needs amputating and we're kids, not vets.'

Then it struck me. How could I be so stupid?

'The hunters! They might have a car somewhere. Or a satellite phone. We could still get her treatment.' I jumped to my feet in excitement.

'Sit down, boyo,' said Blacky. 'It's too late. She's dying. She knows it. She'd be dead before you could get her one kilometre, let alone the hundred to the nearest vet.'

I slumped back down and put my hand very carefully on the tiger's chest. She gazed at me with pain-filled eyes. And it was anger that surged through me then. I could feel it rise from the tiger's skin and tingle through my veins. Anger at what we had done to the world, but also anger at Blacky. It felt hot in my blood.

'But *you* knew about this, Blacky,' I spat. 'You could have told me where she was. I could have told someone. Phil. He'd have saved her.'

115

'Her leg was broken, boyo. It could have been fixed. I only found out about the infection yesterday when I came to bring her food. Remember I said I had an errand? That was it. Bringing her the dried beef I'd stockpiled.'

The explanation wasn't good enough.

'But there was still time,' I cried. 'We could've got a vet here. How could you make that choice, Blacky? To let her die here in agony?'

'It *wasn't* my choice, mush,' said Blacky. 'It was Tess's. She told me that under no circumstances was I to bring anyone but you and Dylan. Her decision. I had to respect that and so must you.'

My anger died then. It dribbled away and in its place was a dark, echoing hole.

'I don't understand, Blacky. What good can I possibly do now?'

'This, tosh.'

He must have said something to the tiger, because she lifted her back leg. She flinched in pain and a thick ooze of pus burst from her wound. But it wasn't the pus that drew my attention. It wasn't even the reek of rotting flesh.

It was the pouch between her legs.

And the three puppies curled within it.

'I belong here,' said Tess. 'This is my world. Not in a cage, pacing to and fro for the rest of my life. Not in a laboratory where I will be cut open, like others before me. When I die, bury me here. Bury me where others of your kind will never find me. Promise.'

Blacky was the go-between. Tess's words appeared in

**116**

my head, but it was his voice I heard.

'I promise,' I said. What else was there to say?

'Thank you. And I ask you to make sure my children – my three beautiful daughters – do not fall into the hands of humans. It would mean their deaths.'

'They'd be looked after,' I said. Humans were bad. But we weren't that bad. The puppies would be raised carefully. Better than most kids. Back from extinction? They would be the royalty of the animal world. Cosseted, pampered, given the best of care.

'You don't understand,' said Tess. 'When others of my kind were captured by humans, they lost the will to live. They never bred in captivity. Not once. Instead, they withered. It might have taken years until they drew their last breath, but they were already dead inside. I don't want that to happen to my children.'

'I'll try,' I said. 'I promise I'll try. But Tess, I'm a kid. I can't raise your daughters by myself. And there are people searching for us. Searching for you, too. I don't know if I can succeed in this.'

I suppose I could have lied. Life was draining from her by the second. I watched, helplessly, as it ebbed away. And maybe it would have been kinder to let her go believing things would turn out okay. But I couldn't. Blacky was right. She deserved respect. She deserved the truth.

'All I ask is that you do your best,' she said. 'But if it cannot be, I have one last request.'

I nodded.

'That you kill my puppies. Quickly. Humanely. And bury them with me.'

She must have seen the horror on my face.

'At least they will have lived and died in freedom,' she continued. 'Promise me.'

I couldn't say anything. I nodded again, but it was just a movement. I was empty inside.

'You are a good person, Marcus. Blacky has told me about you and your friend, Dylan. I would never have wanted my children's fate to be left in the hands of a human, but if it must be so, then I am glad you are the one. I'm glad.'

There was so much I wanted to say, but in the end only one thing meant anything.

'I'm sorry, Tess. I'm so sorry.'

There was a pause.

'She knew that, mush. She knew it.'

I stared at Blacky and then at Tess. Her chest no longer rose and fell. Her eyes were glassy and staring. Whatever lived behind them once had fled.

John Oakman tapped me on the shoulder.

'People,' he said. 'Here.'

The bush covered us. I carefully poked my head out. Two people, maybe a quarter of a kilometre away. Two people buried under a mountain of camping gear. Yup, our tiger hunters might stand out like an Akubra on a polar bear but they had an uncanny knack of being in the wrong place at the wrong time. They were scanning the ground. I wondered for a moment what they were tracking, and then I realised it was us. We'd left a path of beaten grass in our mad run through the bush. Even as I watched, another couple of people appeared from a slightly different direction.

Jimmy and Mr Crannitch. They headed towards us as well.

We ducked back behind the shrub. Brilliant! Fantastic! Of all times to get company, this had to be the worst. I estimated we had five or six minutes before certain discovery. At least it gave me another problem to focus on. I was grateful to

put Tess's last words out of my mind for a while.

'They mustn't find us, guys,' I said. 'If anyone has any brilliant ideas how we're going to get out of this, now would be a good time to share them.'

No reply. Dyl scratched his head. John was still processing the request. If I waited until he understood what was required, we'd be back on the mainland establishing a Guinness Book of Records entry for longest grounding in history. For once, there was nothing from Blacky. Four of us and not even a glimmering of an idea.

'A decoy,' I said, more to myself than anything. 'We need something to attract their attention, get them to move away from here.'

And even as I said it, the idea popped up like one of those light-bulb-over-the-head moments. It was brilliant. It was magnificent. It was the product of a mind bordering on genius.

'No way, mush,' came Blacky's voice in my head. 'I have my dignity, you know.'

'Oh yeah?' I replied. 'Dignity, huh? And rolling in poo helps that how?'

'You might not consider it dignified, tosh, but believe me, among my own kind, I'm considered the very height of refinement.'

'Never mind, Blacky. Time is ticking and this is something you *have* to do. Anyway, you're built for it.' I examined him carefully and nearly reconsidered. Blacky is dirty-white, small, with a stumpy tail and a black patch over one eye. He actually *wasn't* built for this. Then again, maybe we had time to effect a makeover…

As Blacky read my mind, he took a step backwards and I realised I'd have to argue later. I jumped forward and pinned the squirming mutt to the ground.

'Quick, Dyl. Hold Blacky down,' I said. I was treated to a close-up of one of Blacky's rolling eyes. *Master of disguise?* I thought. *Time to put your money where your mouth is, tosh.*

Dyl wasn't keen. He had plenty of experience with Blacky and knew that in a toss-up between confronting a bad-tempered, flick-knife-wielding death adder or tackling the foul-smelling hound, the snake was the wiser option. He did it, though.

'John,' I said once my hands were free. 'I need a short length of your parachute cord and a small branch from that shrub.'

Luckily, John was quicker when it came to practical matters than with concepts. I had a small piece of cord and a half-metre of branch within seconds. Of course, tying the branch to Blacky's tail wasn't very easy. He's only got a short stump of a thing—

'Oi, tosh. Watch your mouth. That tail may be challenged in terms of length, but I'm very attached to it.'

—and getting the branch to stay in place rather than dragging along the ground was tricky. In the end, there wasn't time. It would have to do. Then I spat into the dirt and mixed it around with my fingers. The fifteen stripes I made across Blacky's back and flanks weren't chocolate brown, but they were dark. I sat on my heels and examined my handiwork.

Blacky wasn't a dead ringer for a Tasmanian tiger. He was

too small for one thing. And entirely the wrong colour. In fact, he looked like a small dirty-white dog with a branch stuck on his tail doing a totally putrid impersonation of a pygmy zebra. But I was banking on the hunters getting carried away by the moment.

Dyl let Blacky go. I noticed he kept his hands well away from the dog's jaws, which, under the circumstances, was wise. But Blacky had apparently come to accept that my plan had merit, even if it dented his self-esteem.

'I want you to know that if you ever spread this story, tosh, you're dead.' I cocked *my* head this time. 'I dumped on your doona once,' he continued. 'Next time it'll be your face.'

'*Very* refined,' I replied. 'Now go, Blacky. Run like the wind.'

I peered through a small gap in the bush. The hunters were no more than twenty metres away and heading straight towards us. Everything now depended on Blacky's acting skills and the hunters being complete bozos. As it turned out, I needn't have worried about either.

When Blacky leaped out from behind the bush, the hunters halted as if they'd stood on garden rakes and been smacked between the eyes by the handles. Fear and confusion spread across their faces, quickly followed by waves of excitement and joy. I could almost read their minds.

*A Tasmanian tiger! Finally! Okay, it looks like a pale and ugly runt with dodgy stripes and foliage sticking out its bum, but it's got to be a tiger!'*

George fumbled for his camera while Blacky stood and gave a clear view of his stripes. He even tried to wag his branch but I think it must have been too heavy. Then he took off into the long grass. The hunters yelped and gave chase. It was easy to see where Blacky was heading. The swaying of the grass showed his every movement. But he wasn't content with that. Every fifty metres or so he jumped into the air. I don't think his new tail helped much, because he wasn't very aerodynamic. But each time his squat body appeared over the top of the grass, George and Gloria nearly pooped their pants in excitement and redoubled their efforts to catch him.

It was Blacky's finest moment.

I vowed that, when this was all over, I'd present him with an Oscar for Best Small Dog with a Branch Stuck Up Its Bum Impersonating a Tasmanian Tiger Impersonating a Wallaby.

Somehow, I reckoned the shortlist for this category wouldn't be too long.

He disappeared over the brow of a hill. Within moments the hunters had also vanished, along with the sound of clashing pots and pans. I let out a long sigh. Success!

Then I peered through the bush again.

Failure!

Maybe Jimmy and Mr Crannitch weren't fooled. Maybe they didn't care. Whatever, they were still heading straight for us. I buried my head in my hands. I gave up. I was tired and out of ideas. I was only dimly aware, through my dark, depressing fog, of Dyl and John whispering to each other.

Dyl touched my arm.

'Down to you now, mate,' he said. 'Catch you later.'

Then he and John jumped out from the bush and ran

into the knee-high grass. This time, it was Jimmy and Mr Crannitch who halted in their tracks as if they'd struck an invisible wall.

'Hey, Jimmy, ya hairy Scottish balloon,' yelled Dyl. 'You can kiss our spotty butts!'

And he and John dropped their dacks and mooned them.

There was silence. It was certainly a day for bizarre sights. I don't know which was more surprising, the vision of Dyl's and John's bums reflecting the pale sunlight or the way Jimmy's and Mr Crannitch's jaws crashed onto their boots. But, in a few seconds, Dyl and John had gathered in their rear ends and legged it into the distance.

Jimmy and Mr C continued acting like stunned mullets and then gave chase. Jimmy was super-fit. You could see his bandy legs, heavy with hair and muscle, whirring like a demented fan. Mr C trailed behind, weaving slightly as he followed.

John and Dyl, I reckoned, would eventually be caught. Jimmy might be old but I got the impression he had staying power and lungs like high-performance pistons. They'd bought me time, though. Within a minute I was alone in the landscape.

Alone that is, except for a battered body at my feet and three small bundles of life.

You will have to take my word for it, but the body of a tiger is heavy. Particularly when it has three young still attached. It took all my strength to lift Tess. My knees buckled under the strain. But I had to move her. The spots of dried blood would probably disappear in a day or two, washed away by rain, but I couldn't take the chance of someone discovering the evidence if I buried her there.

I had a promise to fulfil.

I stumbled through the bush for maybe an hour. I had to stop often and shift Tess's weight in my arms, which felt like they'd been injected with lead. After a while I didn't even notice the smell. Sweat stung my eyes. I didn't really have a destination. I just needed to put space between myself and that bush.

Finally, the decision about destination was taken for me. I sagged to my knees and, try as I might, couldn't get to my feet again. This place, wherever it was, would have to do.

I looked around. The trees were sparse but provided some cover. The ground was soft. I placed Tess down carefully and started to dig.

The first ten centimetres was easy. The soil parted between my fingers and I scooped it into a mound. But then it became more difficult. There were roots crisscrossing the forest floor and I couldn't snap them. I sat and wiped my forehead with one muddy hand. Then I opened my backpack. Maybe the emergency pack would contain a knife. It didn't. But I found a metal mug and dug with that. It couldn't get through the roots but, little by little, I made space.

Depth was the key. I didn't want her body dug up by predators. I remembered what I'd read about Tasmanian devils. They were carrion feeders and would eat the bodies of anything they found. I couldn't remember if they would dig to find food, but I wasn't prepared to take the chance. Centimetre by slow centimetre I dug.

'Need a hand, mush? Or should I say a paw?'

I was so tired I could barely lift my head.

Blacky had lost the tail. All that springing around like a jack-in-the-box must have dislodged it. Most of his stripes had disappeared, too. A small image from Blacky's mind popped into mine. A dog on its back, rubbing and writhing against coarse grass. He looked like himself again and I was pleased to see him.

Blacky jumped into the small hole I'd dug and gave it some with his front paws. A cloud of dirt sprayed between his hind legs. I shuffled out of the firing line, rested my head against Tess's and watched. Within ten minutes the hole had swallowed Blacky but he continued digging. After a while, I dragged myself over and scooped away the dirt falling back into the grave.

Later, I carefully took the pups from Tess and laid them on the ground. They snuggled together, their thin stripes merging.

Then I placed Tess into the dark depths of the hole.

I was too exhausted to feel more grief. Or maybe I was so steeped in sorrow I no longer had the means to express it. At any rate, my eyes were dry. I took one last look at her curled body, snug in its final resting place and felt I *should* say something. But I couldn't think of anything. I was empty.

'Sorry,' I whispered once more. But it didn't feel like enough. Not nearly enough. I started to fill the hole.

Afterwards, Blacky and I stared at the mound. Maybe I should have felt pleased with myself. I had done part of what Tess had asked. But as I gazed at the small, squirming forms of her children, I felt only despair.

'I can't take these pups with me, Blacky,' I said. 'And I

certainly can't kill them. I know I made a promise to their mother, but I can't keep it. I have no choice.'

'There's always a choice, mush.'

'You're right. If I gave the pups to the scientists, they'd look after them. Maybe clone them. The species could survive.'

'Tess specifically said no to that, tosh.'

'But Tess didn't consider the alternatives,' I argued. 'She was in pain, not thinking straight. Even if I managed to successfully hide them – and there's no chance of that – bring them up somehow to adulthood, they are females. I can only offer them death. Scientists could offer life.'

Blacky rested his head on my leg. At any other time I would have been amazed at this show of affection but I was too tired, physically and emotionally, to feel anything.

'I understand if you can't do it, Marc,' he said. 'Maybe it's best if it's me. I'll make it quick. They won't feel a thing.'

I burst into tears.

'No, Blacky,' I wailed. 'I can't bear it.'

'Then look away, tosh.'

'What about the pups' father?' I cried. I was desperate enough to clutch at any straw, though I knew Tess and Blacky wouldn't have overlooked anything so obvious.

'Dead.' He paused. 'Come on, Marc. Take a walk. I'll find you when it's all over.'

'No,' I said. I dried my eyes and got to my feet. A cold resolve filled me. 'That's not happening. There's been too much death. I'll stay here with them. I'll hide out in the Tasmanian bush. You can bring food for all of us. *We* can be their mother and father. It's not impossible. We're resourceful. And in a couple of years I can go home.'

'You can't be serious, mush,' said Blacky. 'There's no way you can survive out here.'

I gazed into the forest. My new home. *There are worse places to live*, I thought. Then I remembered our trek through the night and the scuttling of unseen things in the dark. Fear pricked my skin.

'Oh, but I *am* serious, Blacky,' I whispered. 'Deadly serious.'

I pitched my tent in a dense part of the forest.

I would have preferred a clearing, close to a river, but I couldn't take the chance of being spotted. As the sun went down, the cold gathered and seeped into my bones. I couldn't light a fire in case a search party caught its flickering through the bush. So I crawled into the tent with the three pups and tried to ignore my stomach cramping with hunger.

Blacky had gone to fetch his store of dried beef. He'd argued, but I was having none of it. The tiger pups must be starving, and under the circumstances I was prepared to become a meat eater again. Blacky told me he would be at least six hours getting the food. I thought I'd be fine for that length of time. After all, I was prepared to be alone out here for a couple of years, so six hours would be easy.

It wasn't.

Darkness brought out those peculiar snufflings and scratchings from the surrounding bush. No light. Eerie sounds. I felt very small and very afraid.

And it was so cold, I lifted up my sweater and allowed the pups close to my skin where they huddled for warmth. It was a strange feeling. But good.

Until one of them decided I was its mother and tried to find out where the milk was stored.

Have you ever been nipped in the chest by a small Tasmanian tiger? Take it from me, it does nothing to improve your mood when you're cold, hungry and frightened.

'Owwww!' I moaned. It held on for grim death and I had to pry its mouth open, detaching its jaws gently from my skin. 'I'm calling you Tonia,' I said. 'Because when she gets her teeth into you it's almost impossible to shake her free as well.'

I put Tonia down and removed her sisters from under my sweater. I fastened the flaps of the tent firmly and tried to settle down to sleep. The time would pass quicker if I managed to grab a few zeds. And sleep would be a way of quieting my hunger pains until Blacky got back. So I lay my head on a mound of earth, closed my eyes and tried to ignore the scuffling of the pups as they played together. I might even have succeeded in dozing if another ant hadn't scurried into my left nostril.

Maybe it was the same ant as before. Maybe it had taken legal advice and decided my eviction order wasn't worth the paper it wasn't written on.

I sat up and evicted it again. Obviously my movement signalled to the pups that I was desperate for fun, because one immediately slipped up the leg of my jeans and chowed down on my ankle. I rolled up my jeans and pried her loose. It wasn't Tonia. This one had paler stripes.

'Owwww,' I moaned. 'I'm going to call you Rose. She's got a thing for ankles too.'

*Two years*, I thought. Two years of sleepless nights, very little food and being gradually eaten by three tiger pups. On the plus side, it was better than spending the time with my sister.

Blacky returned in the middle of the night. He had the decency to announce his arrival in my head. I couldn't have coped with another mysterious sound or snuffling at the tent flaps. I was close to the end of my tether. I let him in and he dropped a mound of dried beef onto the floor.

'Here we go, mush. Dig in. Boy, that was a helluva journey. I'm pooped.'

I picked up a piece of dried beef while the pups fought over the rest. It disappeared in ten seconds. The beef smelled pretty bad and it was coated in a film of Blacky's saliva. Suddenly I lost my appetite and dropped the piece to the floor, where Rose snaffled it. I sighed.

'How long till dawn, Blacky?' I asked.

'What am I, a speaking clock? Settle down, you twonk, and get some sleep.'

I tried. I might even have succeeded for a few minutes. The pups had quietened down after their meal and lay curled together in the corner of the tent. Blacky snored. I drifted off …

And was woken by the foulest stench I'd ever experienced. And, trust me, I've experienced a few.

'BLACKY!' I yelled. 'That is absolutely disgusting!'

'Not me, boyo,' came the reply. 'Take my word for it, that is so incredibly fruity I would be proud to claim it. But integrity

is my middle name. I cannot take credit for someone else's achievement.'

I sat up. Moonlight must have struggled through the forest canopy, because I could make out the tent's interior. Two pups had separated themselves from the other, who sniffed at her bum and blinked. Even in the poor light I could see this wasn't either Tonia or Rose.

'I don't believe it,' I gasped. 'Nothing that small could produce a smell that big.'

'Aaaah,' sighed Blacky. 'What a talent! Reminds me of when *I* was a pup. I tell you, it's a privilege to be present at the start of a magnificent career ...'

I opened the tent's flaps and wafted furiously. The farting pup seemed very pleased with itself.

'I'm going to call you Becky,' I spluttered.

It was the closest girl's name I could get to Blacky.

I staggered out of the tent into a frozen morning. I was so hungry I could feel my stomach juices digesting my intestines. A pale mist swirled along the ground. Blacky joined me in the bitter air. Tonia, Rose and Becky followed, stretching the sleep from their muscles.

'I'm lighting a fire, Blacky,' I said. 'I don't care anymore. Unless I get some heat I'm going to freeze to death.'

'That's if you don't starve to death first, tosh.'

'Thanks for the cheerful thought.'

'Come on, Marc,' said Blacky. His voice, for once, was gentle. 'This isn't going to work. You know it isn't. How long do you think you can continue like this? Cold, starving, away from your own kind. It's been one night. One night,

Marc. And you really think you can do this for another six hundred or so? Come on. Give it up.'

'I can't, Blacky,' I said. 'I just can't.'

'It will be a miracle if you survive a week.'

He was right. I knew that.

A miracle. I badly needed a miracle.

I gazed around at the hostile bush. It seemed so dark, so lacking in warmth and life.

And then, right at that moment, I sensed, rather than saw, a flicker of movement. Something – something alive – was detaching itself from the forest's shadows.

Two adult thylacines moved between the trees. Their stripes were clearly printed, their tails rigid, their legs strangely stiff in movement, like old people with painful joints. They stood for a moment, wisps of mist playing around their legs. The tiger puppies bounded over to them, playful, uttering strange yips. The adults dipped their heads and sniffed at the pups. Then the female – I imagined it was the female – snuffled at the small forms, picked up Tonia and Rose by the scruffs of their necks. The male took Becky.

We gazed at each other for a few moments. A small boy, a dirty-white dog and five Tasmanian tigers separated by less than a metre. Finally, unhurriedly, they turned and walked back into the forest. I watched as, dappled briefly by pale rays of sunlight, their forms mingled with shadows and the darkness swallowed them.

I watched the empty forest for a full minute until Blacky nuzzled at my arm.

'Come on, tosh,' he said. 'It's time to go home.'

We had our miracle.

The search party found me half an hour later.

Blacky sniffed them out and led me directly into their path. At the last moment he melted into the landscape and I faced them alone. I didn't recognise any of the people, but it was obvious they were looking for me. Guys in jackets with logos on them. There was even a dog. It must have been nosing out my scent. I was exhausted, starving and dehydrated. I couldn't even feel much joy at being safe again.

They half-carried me to a four-wheel drive a kilometre or so away. As soon as I was in the back of the car and it started its bumpy ride I fell asleep. When I came to, I was back in the Wilderness Camp.

I brushed sleep from my eyes and peered through the grimy window at the familiar buildings and the familiar gathering of boys and instructors. Phil was there. Jimmy and Mr Crannitch were back. So were Dyl and John Oakman.

But there was another group of people who didn't belong.

My heart sank as I saw Mum, Dad and Rose.

Boy, was I in trouble.

Mum hugged me so tightly I thought I'd suffocate. Killing me seemed a strange way of showing joy that I was still alive. Mind you, even if she didn't kill me now because I was alive, she'd kill me later for having made her think I was dead.

I confused myself with this line of thinking, so I stopped. It took enough energy just to get air through the folds of her cardigan. When she finally let go I gulped in a deep lungful and prepared for the onslaught.

'Marcus,' she said. 'I was worried sick. We all were.'

'Sorry, Mum,' I breathed. I was, too. I suppose I should have realised my parents would come to Tassie when they heard I'd gone missing. They must have been here for a day and a half. It was obvious I was on the point of being grounded, certainly until I was fifty. Maybe until I could draw my pension. Possibly until four years after my death in 2104.

'Never mind "sorry", Marcus,' said Mum. I closed my eyes. This is where the emotional torture would begin. 'It is *you* who is owed an apology.'

'What?' I blinked open my eyes.

'Dylan. What have you and your friend got to say?'

Dyl and John Oakman stepped forward.

'Sorry, Marc,' said Dyl. He winked at me, very carefully. I don't think anyone else saw it. 'I'm sorry for kidnapping you and taking you off into the bush as a childish prank. It was silly of me and John. We should have known better. But we *are* part of the special boys unit and I guess this is the kind of behaviour you'd expect from dropkicks like us.'

'But ... but ...' I spluttered. 'But— owww!'

'Sorry, Mucus,' said John, withdrawing his boot after it had made violent and bone-crunching contact with my ankle. 'Me bad. Me drongo.'

What was going on? My brain felt like it had been stuck in a washing machine on the fast spin cycle. John stepped back and Mr Crannitch appeared. His eyes were not bloodshot anymore. I was glad he had recovered from his illness.

'I can assure you, Mrs Hill, that the school will not tolerate reckless behaviour. I believe Dylan and John did not fully understand the consequences of their actions. They thought it would be funny to tie up and blindfold your son and lead him into the bush in the middle of the night. I also believe them when they say that getting lost was not part of their plan. But that does not excuse them. Both boys will be severely punished when we return to school.'

Mum looked Dyl up and down.

'I am disappointed in you, Dylan,' she said. 'I thought you were Marcus's friend.'

Dyl lowered his eyes.

'Sorry, Mrs Hill,' he muttered.

That put paid to the Wilderness Camp. I was given something to eat, a couple of cheese sandwiches that I couldn't quite finish despite being starving. They made me feel sick.

Everyone else packed, ready for departure. I was surprised there were no complaints. Later, Dyl explained that the special boys were used to good times ending because of someone's bad behaviour. It was simply a fact of life.

I felt bad about that later.

I had a shower. It felt as though it wasn't just two days'

worth of dirt that swirled down the plughole, but also my tiredness. I felt refreshed. My brain had reported for duty. I had questions that needed answering.

Luckily, I didn't have to wait long. As I was drying my hair, Dyl and John entered the toilet block.

'Guys,' I said. 'What's with this kidnapping business?'

Dyl sat on one of the wooden benches and pulled a can of cola from his jacket.

'We figured there was no point all of us being in the brown stuff,' he said, popping the ring-pull. 'So when Jimmy and Mr Crannitch caught us, we told them we'd carried you off as a joke.'

'But why, Dyl? It was *me* that got *you* guys involved in this. If anyone had to take responsibility it was me, not you.'

Dyl took a drink and passed the can to John.

'No biggie,' he said. 'Me and John are used to being blamed for everything. That's the way it is. You, on the other hand, are a superstar goody-two-shoes sook. No offence, mate.'

'None taken,' I said.

'So it seemed ... *right*, I guess, that we took the blame. We'll probably cop a suspension. Wow, that's a real worry!' His voice dripped with sarcasm. 'And a lecture on responsibility. Small price to pay, mate.'

'But I left a message in the dirt,' I pointed out. 'Saying we were safe. How did that fit in with you guys kidnapping me?'

'Rubbed it out, Mucus,' said John. 'When I followed you. Get you in trouble. Sorry.'

I looked from one to the other. I still had a lot to work out.

'But Mum now thinks you're an irresponsible idiot, Dyl,' I said. 'That's not fair. She likes you.' *Liked you*, I thought.

Sadness flashed into his eyes for a brief moment.

'Yeah, well. That's the only thing that bothers me. But she'll get over it. I hope.'

I turned to John.

'And you, John,' I said. 'I don't understand. You hate me, yet you're prepared to protect me. It doesn't make sense, particularly since you've no idea what all that stuff in the forest was about.' I glanced at Dyl, who shook his head. He hadn't told John anything. I wasn't surprised. If Dyl gives his word, you can take it to the bank.

John's forehead creased in concentration. I got a crick in the neck just watching it.

'No idea, true,' he grunted. 'But normal. Never know what's going on.' His forehead cleared. 'Had fun. Good enough for me.'

'I still think I should tell the truth,' I said.

'You can be so dumb sometimes, Marc,' said Dyl. 'What good would that do? Let it go, mate. Let it go.'

And when I thought about it, I could see the logic. It wouldn't change anything. It might even make it more difficult in the future if Blacky had other missions for us.

I looked at Dyl and John. Dyl was my best mate and I knew he'd do anything for me. But John was a different story. We weren't friends. We were enemies.

I remembered what Dyl told me, back on that first day. The special boys unit was labelled as worthless. Everyone thought so, including the boys themselves. Yet, when you dug beneath the surface, there was a rich vein of goodness there. Kindness, compassion, mateship. I'd been too willing to judge John. I'd got it wrong.

Dyl was right. I was dumb sometimes. More than sometimes.

'Thanks, guys,' I said. 'I won't forget this.'

Dyl pulled out another can of cola.

'Don't thank me, mate,' he said. 'It was John who came up with the whole idea.' He took my arm and dragged me a few metres away. 'Anyway,' he whispered, 'if you want to be grateful, you can tell me what happened back there after we left.'

So I told him about the miracle.

Mum and Dad didn't let me travel with the boys in the bus. They'd hired a car in Tassie and I was forced to sit in the back with Rose as we made the journey to East Devonport. Under most circumstances, this would have been dangerous, but Rose had undergone a transformation.

Normally, this happens during full moons when she develops sharp, pointed canines, a Jimmy-like hair covering and a thirst for blood. My blood. This time, though, it was even scarier.

She was nice to me.

She was considerate.

She was loving.

Yuck.

'You're my little brother, Marcus,' she'd gushed. 'I was soooo worried about you!'

Yeah, right. Worried she'd have no one to torture. Worried there'd be no one whose life she could make miserable. I tried to spot the old, familiar glint of evil in her eye, but it wasn't there. It had been replaced with a mushy soup of tenderness. That was more terrifying than anything I'd been through on this trip.

Someone or something had stolen my sister.

I stood at the front of *The Spirit of Tasmania* and let the wind blow through my hair.

I needed a bit of alone time. I'd had no opportunity to think through what had happened out there in the bush. It had been a miracle and I guess a miracle was bound to leave questions rolling around in my head.

Actually, there was something rolling around in my stomach as well. I'd eaten a hearty breakfast of fried mushrooms and scrambled eggs. Now that Bass Strait was getting choppy I worried they were going to make a reappearance. I closed my eyes and felt the cool spray on my face.

'Yorright, an' at?' came a familiar voice.

I turned.

'Good, thanks, Jimmy,' I replied. 'You?'

'Fit as a butcher's dog, laddie. Nair better.'

'What are you doing on board? I thought you lived in Tassie.'

'Aye, I do that. A wee bizness trip tae Melbourne, lad. Day or two is all.'

We watched the rolling swell for a few moments. I got the impression Jimmy was leading up to something. I waited.

'Oot there i' the boosh, son,' he said finally. 'Do ye feel like talkin' aboot it?'

'Not really, Jimmy,' I said. 'I'm not ready.'

He nodded. 'Aye. I ken whit yer sayin'. Must've bin real scary. Still, though…'

'What?'

'Kinda strange, d'ye no think?'

I waited.

'You bein' a smart wee bairn an' all. Pickin' up them survival techniques real quick. Then, dumped i' the boosh by yer best mate, wanderin' lost fer over twenty-four hoours. And yet, all them bahmpots, the tiger hunters, were aroond. No' tae mention search parties, helicopters. Must've bin a thousand tae one they missed ye, what wid you yellin' for help an' that. As, of course, ye wud've done. Ah mean, laddie, if ye didnae know better, yud think yer didnae *want* to be found. Know what ah mean, eh?'

I said nothing. Jimmy sucked on the inside of his mouth and gazed out to sea.

'Aye, it's a wee mystery, so it is. But, yer ken what I think, son? I think mebbe some mysteries are best kept to yersen. If yer conscience is clear, of course.'

I nodded.

'Cooeee!'

The call came from behind us. We turned.

'Fer cryin' oot loud, son. It's them mad rocket mental numpties. Ah'm ootay 'ere, so I am.' He clapped me on the back. 'Look efter yersen, laddie, eh? Look efter yersen.'

'Thanks, Jimmy. You too.'

And he scuttled through the nearest door. I smiled. *Never underestimate anyone*, I thought. *Especially a gibberish-talking orang-utan impersonator.*

Gloria and George joined me at the front of the boat. They looked very different without camping gear. Smaller, for one thing. Gloria's smile was still a wonder to behold, though. It nearly joined up at the back of her head, exposing a miniature, but dazzling, Stonehenge. I wondered if she'd had to apply for planning permission for those teeth.

'You're the boy who got lost, aren't you?' she said. 'One of those boys on the camp.'

'That's me,' I said. 'And you're the tiger hunters. How did you get on?'

Gloria put a hand over her heart.

'You won't believe it!' she gasped.

'Almost certainly not,' I replied.

'Do you want to see something that will take your breath away?'

I nodded.

George handed her a camera. She turned it on and showed me the image on the LCD panel.

The picture wasn't crystal clear, but I could make out enough details. They'd caught Blacky at the top of one of his leaps. The branch was clear. I spotted a leaf tickling his bum. I was really pleased with the stripes. It was a good job. But, for all that, he looked like what he was. A small, ugly dog. I smiled.

'You know what this is, don't you?' Gloria said.

'I think so,' I replied.

'A Thy-la-cine.'

'Isn't that modelling putty?'

She ignored me.

'This photograph is worth a lot of money,' she continued.

They were so intent on examining every detail of the image that Gloria didn't notice me slip a packet of cheese and tomato sandwiches into her jacket pocket.

I'd bought them earlier, just in case.

'You probably wouldn't be able to guess how much,' she sighed.

'I think it's priceless,' I said.

I stayed on deck. The sea was becoming rougher by the minute and my best chance of avoiding illness was to keep airflow through my lungs. Melbourne was a smudge on the horizon when the sea reached its roughest point.

I was cold and wet and looking forward to my warm, cosy bed. But something was definitely still stirring within me. I recognised the signs and fought it.

There was a tap on my shoulder. So much for quiet time. It appeared the entire world wanted to have a word with me. I turned.

'I just want to say that I am sooo glad to have you back, Marcus,' said Rose. 'I've missed you.'

But I didn't miss her.

She copped the entire contents of my stomach.

As Rose wiped diced carrots from her eyes, I caught a glimpse of that familiar glint. The sharp edge of hatred. The gleam of violence. The thirst for revenge. Even as I ran for cover, I couldn't help but smile.

Someone had returned my sister and it was good to have her back.

That didn't mean I was going to let her catch me, though. The scars on my ankle were only just beginning to fade. I raced through the ship's corridors, Rose close on my heels. I could feel her breath on the back of my neck. Being coated in vomit certainly hadn't slowed her down. In fact,

I was beginning to accept that she was certain to catch me when I spotted the door to the gents' toilets.

I made it through with only centimetres to spare. For a moment I thought she'd come in after me. But then I heard her fist against the door and a few hoarse promises of what she'd do to me when I came out.

Like I was going to come out! I could stay here until we docked. I went into one of the cubicles, locked the door and sat on the toilet seat. Safe! I took a deep breath.

And nearly threw up. Again!

'BLACKY!' I yelled. 'What have you rolled in now?'

'Nothing, tosh,' came the voice in my head. 'I have given up rolling in stuff. I considered what you said about it being inconsistent with my dignity and, though I never thought I'd say this, you might be right. So, hard though it is, I have already turned my back on a delectable pile of wallaby poop and a mound of vintage vixen vomit.'

He squirmed out from the back of the toilet bowl and sat in front of me. I fixed him with a glare.

'So, the smell, Blacky?'

'Straight from my bum, bucko. Aaaah. I'm back!'

I sighed.

'Blacky? There's only one thing I don't understand.'

'I find that impossible to believe, tosh. Based on my experience, it's *most* things you don't understand.'

I ignored him. It's easier that way.

'I thought Tess was the last of the tigers. Where did those other two come from?'

'No idea, mush. I thought she was the last remaining adult. Thankfully, we were wrong. And it's not often *I'm*

wrong. In fact, I can't think of another instance …'

I paid no attention to his bragging. I was remembering that nightmare in the tent. The glimpse of a long snout, the shadowy movement against the night. It made more sense now.

'The future might not be so bleak,' he continued. 'Even if those two adults are the last of their kind, there is a chance. Those three pups, when they've grown to maturity, will bring new genes into the pool. Touch and go, tosh. But if they can avoid humans, they may yet survive as a species. You should be proud.'

I was. I couldn't tell anyone, of course. But it was enough for me and Dyl to know what we'd helped to achieve. It felt good. It felt really good.

'I'm off as soon as we dock, mush,' said Blacky. 'Things to see, people to do. The life of an eco-warrior is a busy one, and I am much in demand around the globe as an authority.'

I had visions of Blacky in a lecture room, giving a Power-Point presentation to the President of the United States. He'd need to fumigate the premises afterwards, mind. Talk about toxic waste.

'Next time, eh, Blacky?' I said.

'Count on it, tosh,' he said. 'Count on it.'

## ABOUT THE AUTHOR

BARRY JONSBERG was born in Liverpool, England, and now lives in Darwin, Australia with his wife, children and two dogs – Jai and Zac, neither of whom, thankfully, share Blacky's flatulence problems.

*Blacky Blasts Back: on the tail of the Tassie tiger* is Barry's third book for younger readers and is a follow-up to *The Dog That Dumped on My Doona* and *A Croc Called Capone*. He has also written several novels for young adults, all of which have been published to great acclaim. *The Whole Business with Kiffo and the Pitbull* was shortlisted for the CBC Book of the Year (Older Readers) in 2005. His second book, *It's Not All About You, Calma!* won the Adelaide Festival Award for Children's Literature and was shortlisted for the CBC Book of the Year (Older Readers) in 2006. *Dreamrider* was shortlisted for the 2007 NSW Premier's Award (Ethel Turner Award). Another novel for older readers, *Ironbark*, was published in June 2008, followed by *Cassie* in November 2008.

During a visit to Tasmania, Barry fell in love with the place and hungered for a glimpse of a Tassie tiger. Unfortunately it didn't happen, but he holds out hope that somewhere in the remote areas of that beautiful island, a family of tigers is living in peace and avoiding humans.

'DEVIOUSLY ENJOYABL
BOOKSELLER + PUBLISHER

THE DOG THAT DUMP
ON MY DOONA

BARRY JONSB

A CROC CALLED CAPONE

BARRY JONSBERG

READ ALL ABOUT
MARCUS & DYL'S
PREVIOUS MISSIONS!